HOLLYSTONE HEARTS: GLENNA

BY

ANN STAADT

PublishAmerica
Baltimore

ISBN: 1-60672-508-4
PUBLISHED BY PUBLISHAMERICA, LLLP
www.publishamerica.com
Baltimore

Printed in the United States of America

Hollystone Hearts: Glenna is dedicated with love to my daughters-in-law, Mary Ruth Staadt and Candy Sue Staadt.

Special thanks go to Ann Wintrode, Judy Post, and the Summit City Scribes for their help in editing this book.

PublishAmerica Titles by Ann Staadt

A New Moon for Emily
Claire in Love
The Reluctant Cowboy
The Light in the Tunnel
The Woman in the Blue Mercedes
Hollystone Hearts: Glenna

Other titles:

Lily Brightfeather

CHAPTER 1

I ran right into him! When I hit his well-muscled chest the impact knocked the breath out of me. If the fellow hadn't grabbed me, I'd have fallen. I felt as if I'd slammed into a brick building at 40 miles an hour. I overslept and was rushing to the opening session of *Dramatic Designs for the Daring Decorator*. After dashing down a long hallway in Caesar's Palace Hotel, you know the one in Las Vegas, I turned a corner and smashed into the guy.

I struggled to get air in my lungs and when I'd drawn in a couple of breaths, I looked up at the tall fellow who'd saved me. Worry creased his face but then he smiled at me and I received the impression of great charm. His deep blue eyes crinkled at the corners. A thatch of streaked blond hair fell on his forehead and he glowed with appeal. It might turn into a heart-stopping romantic encounter if only I could breathe.

I looked down and saw alligator cowboy boots on his feet and expected to hear Texas or Oklahoma in his voice. It bowled me over when he spoke. "I say, miss, are you all right? I'm most awfully sorry to have run you down." The man sounded British!

Unable to speak, I nodded my head and wondered how I'd gotten into this situation. He stood there holding me up in that ridiculous hallway, which looked like a rummage sale at the Forum. He deftly slid an arm around my waist and plopped me down on a chunk of concrete that looked to be a souvenir from the Roman Coliseum. "Now then, miss, you're alarmingly pale."

I struggled to stand. "I'm okay. I must get to a meeting." It seemed vitally important for me to attend the opening session of the convention and hear the keynote address.

He gently pushed me back down. "Stay right there. You shouldn't move yet. Ah, I see some pink coming back into your cheeks. Well, if you must stand up, let me assist you. Go slowly, don't move so fast."

"I think I'm all right. I can breathe now." After a minute I squeaked out a few more words. "I'm sorry for knocking you off course. I shouldn't have been in such a hurry. Are you on your way to a convention session?"

He put his hand on my back. It felt warm and comforting. When he spoke I heard that accent again. "I thought about going to a presentation, but there's no rush. Let me see you right and then we'll worry about conferences. Could you do with a coffee? Some breakfast, perhaps?"

"Oh, no! Don't let me delay you. It was all my fault that I body-slammed you. I need to go on to my seminar. Thanks so much for your help." I turned back to look at him again. "Did I hurt you?"

He smiled at me. "I'm right as rain. Now, did you have anything to eat this morning?"

"No, I slept in, but I didn't mean to get up so late. It's really important for me to attend this seminar." I made an effort to smooth a wrinkle out of my green linen suit.

Guy McLeod, the name on his convention tag, whisked me into an elevator and indicated we wanted to go down. I expected the elevator operator to be wearing a toga, considering the decor of the hotel, but he disappointed me.

Guy slipped his arm under mine and gave me some badly needed support. "It doesn't do to skip the morning meal. That's a bad way to start the day. We'll fix you up and don't fret about your meeting. I'll wager the speaker has written a book, which he'll push you to buy. Well, buy it and read what he has to say. Or better still, the conference staff is undoubtedly taping the session. Purchase the tape and enjoy it whenever you want. You can play it over and over again when you get back home."

I must admit I'm easily swayed when masterful men are involved, and I let him lead me to a booth in the hotel breakfast buffet. "Now, coffee?"

I smiled at him. "Tea, please."

"Really!" It wasn't just off-brand restaurant tea he conjured up. I breathed in the fragrance of Bigelow English Breakfast and could feel my condition improve sip by sip.

"Now that you've caught your breath, tell me why's it so important for a beautiful redhead with smashing green eyes to attend this meeting you're missing."

"I'm an interior decorator. I came to this Las Vegas conference because I need to keep abreast of new trends. Just because I love English country décor doesn't mean my clients won't want the latest look in minimalism. It'd be a treat to tackle this hotel. The Roman look is getting a bit tacky. But tell me what your convention is about."

"Ah, well, I've a small investment in oil and these conferences are a place to meet others in the business. I don't need to attend the sessions. The contacts are mostly made at cocktail parties and private meetings."

This man looked so like a Texas oilman in his blue western-cut suit. And yes, the cowboy boots led me astray. He took my arm, steered me to the buffet, and handed me a plate. Then this take-charge man proceeded to heap it with scrambled eggs, bacon, muffins, and fruit.

After he collected his own breakfast, we moved back to the booth. I couldn't resist questioning him. "I'm curious about where you're from? Somewhere in the British Isles, I'd guess."

"I'm from a bit of all over. My accent drives people crazy when they try to place it. I'm a native of Scotland and Mother lives there yet. My parents sent me to an English school which ground away some of my Scottish burr and I've kicked around all over the world in recent years."

"You must lead an exciting life."

He refilled out teacups. "I'd call it more hectic than exciting. Tell me, where do you do this interior decorating you spoke about?"

"I live in Oakbrook, a Chicago suburb. It's a busy, upscale town and the competition is tough. I take on quite a number of offices to refurbish, but I've handled a couple of jobs for people with estate-type homes. I'd love to do more of that."

He looked at me with interest. "Is that what you'd prefer to do? Work on big houses?"

"I love all kinds of decorating but houses are my first love."

When we'd emptied our plates I leaned back to enjoy my last cup of tea. I hated to leave this interesting man, but my livelihood depended on my getting to the decorating convention. I stood and laid ten dollars on the bill. "That should cover my share. I've loved talking to you, but we better go to our meetings. I'm sorry for not slowing down for the corner this morning. You've been so nice and helpful."

The man's face flushed red and he shoved the money away. "Guy McLeod doesn't take a charming young woman out, even for breakfast, and let her pay her own way. There'll be none of that."

"Oh, excuse me," I said. "Th-things are different here. Please don't be offended. I didn't want to take advantage of your kindness."

His high color faded and I could see him take a breath. "It's sad I am to lose my temper with such a charming young lady, but I'd feel a fool if I let you pay for your meal. I've enjoyed the chance to get acquainted with you and would like to see you again. Are you free this evening?"

My mind ran rapidly over the convention schedule and I felt rather shy as I turned to him. "My group has a cocktail hour from six to seven o'clock this evening. You could join me for that."

"Fine. Tell me where and — my word — I don't even know your name."

"Oh, my nametag's in my purse. I left in such a rush this morning. I'm Glenna James. I'll be in the Janiculum Ballroom." I held out my hand. The hand that clasped mine felt warm, and I let myself think ahead to the evening. This could turn out to be an exciting trip. "Thank you again for your help and kindness. I'll see you later."

CHAPTER 2

My day came jam-packed with information. I attended a workshop on color matching where the speaker hammered away at basic information. "It's important to coordinate the colors in a home with the owners' personalities. If you have two people who clash on the color charts, it takes careful planning to bring harmony to their setting." Well, I knew that.

Next I attended *What To Do with those White Walls Left Over from the Last Century.* Obviously, you paint them with the in colors. I did make a note that the in colors for this year were rather fruity — -tart lime, tangerine passion, and frosted blueberry.

The last session of the day featured accessorizing and the presenter did a terrific job. Finally, a speaker on my wavelength. I scribbled down a bushel of good ideas.

As evening approached I stood by the door of the ballroom and scanned the crowd. Decorators I knew, or had met that day, stopped to chat a minute. I'd launched into a discussion on window treatments when a large hand slid under my elbow. A deep voice spoke in my ear. "Miss James, may I get you a drink?"

I looked away from the tiny gal with skinny legs, who talked up at me, and glanced over my shoulder at Guy McLeod. "Tonic and lime, please."

"And can we get you something Miss, Miss —?"

"Annabeth Grimes, and I'd love a drink." She batted extraordinarily long lashes at Guy and twittered at him with a Texas accent. "A dry martini would be wonderful." As he moved through the crowd to the bar, she didn't take here eyes off him. "I so love a man with a British accent. Have you known him long?"

I'm a tough businesswoman, thirty-three years of age. I've been a homeowner for seven years and managed my own business since I turned twenty-five. I keep my cool and rarely give in to anger, but something in her voice lit a bomb in my gut. It was me who bumped into this man and for this evening at least he should be mine. I answered her through gritted teeth. "He's a rather recent acquaintance from Scotland and we planned to meet here tonight."

I hardly know why, but she made me so hot I couldn't think. Why did she have to horn in on our conversation? Guy handed us our drinks, we sipped, and he asked us questions about our day. What an unusual man he seemed. He knew so much about housing for someone who looked to be in his thirties. One would think him to be in the construction business instead of an oilman.

While Annabeth stuck to us as if we wore flypaper we slowly circled the room. What a frightful venue, awash with pale-pink draperies and Roman columns in the most awkward places.

We stopped to say a few words to a woman I knew. "Phyllis Turner, this is Annabeth Grimes and Guy McLeod. Phyllis gave me my first job right out of design school. She has a wonderful salon in Chicago and I learned a lot from her. I didn't know you were coming out for this meeting, Phyl."

Phyllis asked how we enjoyed today's speakers. Miss Yellow-Curls, Annabeth, edged right in, speaking in her high squeaky voice. "It's so excitin' to meet decorators from all over the country. Ah'm from Texas and the folks back home think cowhide upholstery and Indian blankets are high style. I do my best to convert them to somethin' a little more classy."

Phyllis gave me a grin and we agreed to meet the next day for lunch.

When the crowd began to drift away, Guy McLeod proved himself a thoughtful gentleman. "Could I interest you ladies in some food? Let's go find a steak."

Annabeth blinked her baby blues at him and I felt my stomach turn. "Oh, I couldn't impose. You two go ahead."

I breathed a prayer. *Oh, yes, you go on to your room for the night and leave us alone.*

"Nonsense," Guy said, "You must come with us. Let's step outside and I'll whistle up a cab."

He took us each by an arm, whisked us through the huge casino, and found a door out. Little Miss Annabeth's size allowed all three of us to fit easily into the taxi, even though Guy McLeod was a large man with wide shoulders. She was mostly dressed in ruffles, made of what looked like cut-rate rayon curtain material. Her pile of too yellow curls came straight from a bottle.

Something had happened to me. I had no time for jealousy in my life. I tossed my head to lift my hair off my neck and tried to get a grip. Guy appeared to be a nice fellow but I scarcely knew him. He attracted me, but so had heaps of other men.

Several great fellows have come and gone in my life and I've come close to marriage a couple of times, but I've never loved anyone enough to give up my single life. For a litmus test, I check the thoughts racing through my head during a passionate kiss. If, during a steamy embrace, I find myself mentally redoing a kitchen, I know that man won't do for me.

In the restaurant Guy McLeod and I asked for rare steaks. Miss Yellow Curls ordered in her little-girl voice. "Ah'll have a small piece of poached chicken breast."

Guy made a great host. He questioned us about our work and in turn told us a bit about his day's activities. He made the oil business sound fascinating and it intrigued me. "Tell me, Guy, do you buy, sell, or broker oil? Do you prospect for black gold or arrange the drilling?"

"Actually I do all of those things. Right now I have a rig delving away on the east coast of South Africa, in Richardson's Bay. I plan to fly out there at the end of this week. I need to see some folks here in the States first."

When we returned to the hotel, Yellow Curls had the grace to fade away and I boldly invited Guy to my room for tea. We settled into comfortable chairs and drank our room service Earl Gray while enjoying Macadamia nut cookies.

My mother would have produced five kittens on the spot if she'd seen me that night. Nice girls don't let men into their hotel rooms under any circumstances, unless they're engaged. She gives me these mixed messages that I must snag a husband at all costs, but I have to be an extremely nice girl while doing so. Mom hasn't entered the twenty-first century and I doubt she ever will.

It seemed like a good time to find out more about this fellow. "Where in England do you make your home? I took a trip to London once and immediately fell in love with the city, the people, and what little I got to see of the countryside."

"You'll have to come for another, longer visit. I hope this doesn't sound trite, but London isn't the country and England isn't London. I have a house outside the big city and it needs some work, actually a heap of work."

That intrigued me and I wanted to know more. "Does it have a name? I love the British way of naming their homes. Here in America only very wealthy folks hang a handle on their estates. And the rest of the people think they're showing off or being snooty."

He looked at me in puzzlement. "Tell me Glenna, what does 'snooty' mean?"

I couldn't help but laugh. "It means going around with your snoot or nose up in the air. I expect it goes right along with being '*too big for one's britches.*'"

He gave me a warm smile. "You are the most enlightening young lady. If I spent time with you I'd learn all sorts of interesting words and phrases."

"Perhaps, but really, does your house have a name and where is it?" I'd dreamed of visiting a manor house, and maybe even decorating one.

He bit into a cookie and didn't answer for a minute. "The place is called Hollystone House and it's near the village of Upper Halsey. I suppose it's thirty miles from the west edge of London."

"That's interesting. What does your house need? To be redecorated, remodeled, or rebuilt?" I poured out more tea and he added milk to both of our cups.

"You do ask complex, multiple questions, Glenna. I've had the roof and cellars repaired. New plumbing and heating were installed and the kitchen is totally modern except for a dishwasher. Otherwise the house is ready for paint, furniture, and drapes."

"How many rooms does your house have and is it old?"

"It's quite old; sections of it are twelfth century. The great hall is part of the original house. The wings out to the side are early Victorian. Fortunately, the previous owners maintained it well. I'm not sure how large the place is, but I expect Hollystone House has between forty and fifty rooms."

The place sounded better and better. "Forty to fifty rooms! Now that would be a decorating job to sink one's teeth into. Give me a call if you can't find anyone local to take on the job."

Guy looked at me with a gleam in his eye. "I might do that."

I stood up and being a British gentleman Guy politely rose to his feet. "I'm sure we both have busy days tomorrow. Thank you for a wonderful dinner and an interesting evening. Maybe I'll run into you again during the convention."

"Oh, I hope not. One of us might be hurt this time."

"Oh, right." We both laughed. "But you know what I mean. Maybe I'll see you tomorrow."

"Count on it! You will see me again. I don't believe in leaving things to chance, Glenna James. What's your schedule like for the rest of the week?"

"My convention day starts with another early meeting. There's a breakfast speaker and he'll lecture on rehabilitating old structures. Maybe you should join us to find out what your Hollystone House needs."

"What a jolly good idea. Tell me where and what time and I'll be there."

"We're supposed to go through the breakfast buffet line and take a filled plate to the Forum. The lecture begins at eight o'clock."

To hold off any unnecessary moves on Guy's part, I held out my hand, gave his a businesslike shake, and stepped into the hall with him. I felt attracted to him but wasn't about to rush into anything. Maybe I'd try to avoid Annabeth tomorrow. I could do without spending the day in Miss Yellow Curl's shadow. Her squeaky voice made the hair on the back of my neck stand up.

CHAPTER 3

When I walked into the meeting room the next morning, with my plate of fruit and croissants, Guy stood by Annabeth Grimes and appeared to be deep in conversation with her. Miss Yellow Curls, with the tweety-bird legs, had struck again. Why couldn't I get myself out of bed these mornings? We might have avoided her if I'd made it down first. They spotted me and motioned for me to join them.

After we chatted a bit, the program began. The workshop turned out to be of great interest and I took pages of notes. To illustrate his presentation, the speaker used one of those great old houses on the Hudson River, above New York City. Guy seemed intrigued with the slides that accompanied the lecture and afterward he asked a number of questions.

Yellow Curls gushed over him. "Oh, Guy, it is so excitin' that you have a stately home to decorate. It would be a wonderful opportunity to work on a house like yours." I did a slow burn because I wanted the chance to decorate his mansion. Our crash in the hallway should give me some priority with this fellow. Just in case, I quietly wrote down Guy's color preferences and the areas he showed special interest in.

The rest of the week whizzed past. Guy entertained me every evening for dinner. We managed to elude Annabeth after a couple of days, in part because I got out of bed earlier. Beating her to meet Guy gave me a real reason to get up early and it certainly lifted my spirits. Our last night in Vegas I skipped my convention dinner and we did the town. We saw two shows, *Folies Bergere* and later laughed at a wickedly funny comedian.

During our late night dinner I drank too much champagne. Guy kept telling the waiter to refill the glasses. I would giggle, and in minutes the flute was empty again. I avoided getting into too much trouble, but I should be old enough to practice moderation. I wish Mother would quit looking over my shoulder. Most my life I've struggled to get out from under my overbearing parents.

We ended the evening with coffee in a hotel café and I managed to navigate the halls of the hotel and find my room.

As he unlocked my door for me, Guy beamed his blue eyes at me. "May I come in for a while?"

Somehow a ray of good sense crept into my brain. "I'm really tired and have to catch early plane tomorrow morning." I gave him my best smile and prepared to duck into my room. "It's been a great week and I'm glad we met. Thank you for the dinners and good times we've enjoyed together. Goodbye now."

Guy slid his arms around me, pushed open my door with his elbow, and guided me into the room. He planted a powerful kiss on my lips. My mind emptied of revamped kitchens or anything else. While I leaned against the doorjamb and tried to recover a bit, he handed me my key. "I'll be in touch."

Wow!

I crawled into bed and tried to recall his good looks. He stood tall, over six feet by several inches. His wardrobe seemed to contain western cut suits in a variety of colors. I mentally ran down the list of his attributes. A slim torso, an engaging grin, and an easy, relaxed manner certainly made him attractive. The chance of his getting in touch with me seemed remote but I could hope. Maybe I should finally quit resisting my mother and begin to think about marriage and a family.

CHAPTER 4

I managed to get up early enough to catch my plane out of Las Vegas the next morning. I arrived at O'Hare Airport by noon, caught a shuttle bus into Oakbrook, retrieved my van from a hotel lot, and pulled into my driveway by two o'clock.

Home looked good to me after a week of hotel living. It's a big old brick farmhouse, which sits in a welter of new homes. Developers bought the farmland for housing additions and houses sprouted in rows. I grabbed the house minutes before the bulldozers lined up to push it into a pile of rubble.

The two front parlors and the dining room are my design studio. Behind that is the original kitchen, which I modernized, but decorated in a country look. Even with a round oak table and matching chairs, the room is large enough to use as a sitting room. A long, comfy sofa is available for television watching and a rare afternoon nap. The room is decorated in cheerful, early-American colors — that wonderful blue, a faded red, and antique white.

I'd spent the flight enjoying daydreams about a tall, handsome oilman with a British accent but I'd better forget him and get back to reality. I unpacked and threw a load of clothes into the washer, which hides with the dryer in the old pantry. Next, I went through the mail and it pleased me to find some checks for completed decorating jobs.

Two inquiries about future work waited on my answer machine. I returned those calls and set up an appointment to consult with one of them. Finally, I called my parents, who live two suburbs away, to let them know their youngest chick made it home from that den of iniquity out West.

My folks are in their late fifties, rather religious, and they breathe heavily on me. They have an ongoing concern about the state of my sex life. I think they've quit worrying that I'll present them with an illegitimate grandchild, but during my twenties it was their constant fear. Since I've toiled in the work force for eleven and a half years and own my home free and clear, they've transferred some of their attention to my older brother, Michael.

He works as a graphic designer, like Dad. Mother engineered his early marriage to Sarah Marshall the minute he graduated from college. They have three little boys and I am down on my knees grateful that those kids consume so much of my parents' time and energy.

I dutifully reported on the convention, made no mention of tall oilmen from across the pond, and escaped as soon as possible. But first there came the subtle questions. "Did you meet any interesting people, dear?" Read people to mean men.

"Gosh, Mother, the meetings kept me so busy that I only saw decorators. Remember Phyllis, my first boss? Well she came and I really enjoyed getting to see her. And I met this funny little woman from Texas." One thing that really bothers my folks is the fact that a few male decorators are gay. I don't know how Mother thought they could harm me.

Last, I called my dear friend, Moira Fitzgerald. We roomed together in design school and I could wait no longer to tell her about Guy McLeod. "Hi, friend. I'm back and I've met a most interesting man."

"Truly? An eligible man?"

"I really don't know. He could have a wife hidden in Scotland or any number of willing women scattered around the globe. He's an oilman who seems to travel constantly. He doesn't wear a wedding ring. If I hear from him again, then I'll worry about the details. I didn't want to scare him off by being too forward."

"I'm thrilled for you, Glenna. How'd you meet?"

I gave her a rundown on our spectacular crash in the hotel and the activities that followed.

"I knew I should sign up for the convention. He might have come up with a friend for me or at least an acquaintance. If I'd only finished the job for old Mrs. Flockhart in time, I could have gone with you."

Moira works for a large interior-decorating firm in Chicago and has emerged as their top designer. She's better than good and I'm not above making a phone call to pick her brains when I have a dearth of ideas or get stumped with a sticky design problem.

I tried to console her. "There'll be more conventions and plenty of other men to crash into. And this fellow may never give me a call. He said 'I'll be in touch,' but we both know that doesn't mean diddily squat."

"Right. Well, there's still dear old Mason, but he's so dull and predictable. It would be great to meet someone I could get excited about. I wish I'd been born in the era of swashbuckling heroes. Today's pirates do leveraged buyouts and takeovers, like Mason, and it's not the same."

We chatted a bit more and agreed to meet for lunch on the following Friday.

CHAPTER 5

A few weeks after my return from Las Vegas I'd almost finished a large office-decorating project. It wasn't a difficult job because the firm owner turned out to be the typical male. "We prefer something not too contemporary, but we want to look like a modern company. If we go for traditional, the look could turn off our younger clients. What do you suggest?"

I proposed that I come and view their office, do some research, and get back to him in a few days. For people with indefinite ideas and a sneaky desire to straddle two eras I have a standard plan. It sits ready in my files with pictures, colors, and details. I simply wait a while and then call with this wonderful idea. My plan is a combination of traditional and modern. I use straight lines, simple furniture, and rich heavy fabrics.

Wallpaper with architectural detail works well. Most men like blue and combining it with ivory immediately hooks them. And there you have my plan, to which I add a few green plants. If the company CEO seems a bit daring, I incorporate a touch of burgundy in some unobtrusive detail. It works like magic.

The one place I individualize on the plan is with accessories. I hunt for really dazzling pictures or offer to blow up and frame photos of the founding fathers. For this job I created a montage of the corporate officers. Fitting the photos into heavy silver frames, with a thin navy mat, would complete the project.

As I checked over my plan for any omissions, the phone rang. "Glenna, is this Glenna James?"

Guy McLeod actually called me. I felt a thrill whiz from my head to my toes. My heart leaped into my throat, and I barely managed to squeak out a yes.

"I truly enjoyed the time we spent together in that unholy city, Las Vegas. What a delightful companion you were and I'd like to see you again."

"Where are you, Guy?"

"I'm at the airport. I could grab a taxi and meet you anywhere you say. Is there a comfortable old hotel near your home where we could have afternoon tea?"

"I know the perfect place." I gave him directions and then tore upstairs to my bedroom closet. This date called for a stunning outfit. And the best choice hung right in front of me. Last year Mother gave me a green, raw-silk suit for Christmas. I love to wear it because it's figure flattering and one of my favorite colors. I flew around to shower and subdue my thick hair. I opted for the romantic look with my curly locks sweeping my shoulders.

It struck exactly four o'clock when I pulled into the hotel. Guy sat in the lobby reading the *Chicago Tribune*. He leaped to his feet when he saw me, rushed to my side, and planted a tender kiss on my cheek. Before I could say hello he had me seated in an intimate corner of one of the dining rooms. As soon as we connected with the chairs, a waiter delivered tea with luscious little sandwiches and cakes.

Guy oozed charm, just as I remembered. "This entire month I've looked forward to seeing your heart-shaped face again, Glenna. My memory didn't play me false. You're still lovely."

My face flushed with heat and color and I struggled to reply. "Guy, it's wonderful to see you, and the tea goodies look terrific. I believe I forgot to eat lunch today." We chatted about unimportant things until the tiny cakes and mini sandwiches were quite gone. He drained the teapot into our cups and I could tell from the way he settled himself into his chair that something big was coming.

"Glenna, I've a job for you. Will you come to England and decorate Hollystone House for me?"

I'd daydreamed about creating dramatic public rooms and intimate bedrooms in a medium-sized castle, but harbored no expectation it would become reality. Words leaped from my mouth before my brain could engage. "Sure, I'll come over and do the job for you. When do we start?"

"I'm afraid it won't be us. One reason I need a good decorator is that I can't be there to oversee the job during the next few years. That's why I need someone like you to take over. When we talked in Las Vegas, your ideas impressed me. You seem to be the kind of high-energy person who can get the job done. I'll pop in from time to time and keep you steered in the right direction. When would you be free to come?"

"Wait a minute here." The blood rushed to my head and it began to throb. "My smart mouth and I were half kidding when I said I'd come so fast. Are you sure you want me for this job? There must be decorators in England. Is it economically smart to import me? I'm bound to cost more than a local person."

"You may cost more but price isn't the only object. There's compatibility and harmony and several other factors." He smiled warmly at me. "So will you come and make me a lovely home? Perhaps I should list some enticements that may encourage you to accept my offer. I'll give you a weekly salary, rather than pay a percentage of the job, since at this point we don't know how long the job will take. I'll send you a plane ticket, and give you a free hand to hire workers. I would like to discuss costs and styles of furniture before you make any massive expenditures."

"How many rooms are we talking about?"

"There were about thirty-five bedrooms on two floors, but I had some of them made into bathrooms and closets. I'd estimate there are seventeen to twenty bedrooms and each has a bathroom or shares one with the room next door. And there's a separate master bedroom suite on the main floor, north wing. And we mustn't forget the top floor. That's a rabbit warren of tiny quarters that used to house the servants. I couldn't tell you how many cubicles are up there."

"Well, I can see if I'm going to purchase more than a dozen bedroom sets that you might want me to run the costs by you. My heavens, this is going to be the job to end all jobs. I think I better consult an attorney and have him draw up a contract."

"A good idea. Then I'll have my solicitor read your contract and advise me on whether to sign it." Guy flashed me a large smile and looked amused by my reaction to his job offer.

"The place sounds like it could be a small hotel or a country inn."

He gave me a quizzical look. "Who knows what the future will bring. I may give that some thought."

"What time frame do you plan on? By the way, are you an English lord?" He looked at me in surprise.

"No, I'm not an English lord, but in Scotland I'm the Laird of Ramsgate Hill. Are you suitably impressed?"

"I'm terribly flustered. Should I bow to you or simply duck my head? Will I need to wear your family crest on my jeans and T-shirt while I work on the house?"

"Oh, heavens no. I wouldn't want the neighbors to think we were the least bit pretentious or snooty." He winked at me. "Now, if Mother comes to visit, she might want something like that. She could demand you wear the crest on your pinnie. Jeans wouldn't do at all."

My mouth dropped open. "What's a pinnie?"

"It's a pinafore and is considered suitable dress for scullery maids and other domestic household help. Let's talk about time and space now. When will you be free to start on the job?"

"I'm committed to jobs that will last about four weeks. If I don't take on any more work, I'll be free at the end of that time. How long do you figure decorating your home will take?"

Guy thought a while. "Somewhere between one and two years. It will depend a great deal on you. Will you do the painting or hire someone? There is some furniture in the house. Would you refinish it or have the work done? Actually the job will be what you make of it."

"By the time I'd come back, my business would be gone and I'd need to acquire clients all over again. But it's probably worth it."

We both leaned back and thought things over for a time. Then Guy sat up straight and leaned across the table so our faces almost touched. "We've sat here so long it's almost seven o'clock. Can we go someplace and have a celebratory dinner?"

I thought a minute. "How do you feel about Chinese takeout? We

24

could pick up an order and go back to my place. I'd really like to do some work on your project, ask you about colors, and draw up a floor plan of the house. How long will you be here in the Chicago area?"

"My plane leaves at noon tomorrow. I have to go back to South Africa. I'll definitely plan to be in England to meet your plane, take you to the house, and get you started."

"It sounds as if we should do some work now. Let's talk this evening and I'll make notes. Then while I finish my commitments here, I can begin to draw up plans for your house. When I come, you can approve or veto my ideas. How does that strike you?"

"It strikes me very well. Let's pick up some egg rolls and almond chicken and get to work." We got in my van and I called our take-out order into Wing Fay's restaurant on my cell phone. As we coasted to the drive-up window, I assumed I'd pay for the food since we were going to my house.

Guy got red in the face, just like last time, and shoved a twenty toward the window.

I got a little hot too. "You're coming to my office to discuss hiring me to work for you. In this country if you're selling something, as I am selling myself to you right now, I should pay. It's called sweetening the pot."

Guy wouldn't listen to the idea that I was the hostess. He made me feel a bit angry and I reacted by asking for an extra order of Crab Rangoon.

I calmed down a bit and drove toward my house. "Will there be a car or van for me to drive? I'll have to run all over to check on prices and pick up things I've ordered. That's why I have this van. Decorators do a bunch of legwork."

"There's an ancient lorry that belongs to the estate. You can start with that and perhaps we can purchase a van later. Let's see how all this goes first."

"What's a lorry?" I asked.

He gave his charming smile. "Lorry is what we call a truck. This one is a Land Rover that's fitted with a pickup box. I don't know its age because it came with the house. But I promise you it does run. I drove it the last time I checked on the place."

I hustled the laird into my studio, sat him down, and handed him fabric samples to look through with one hand while he ate an egg roll with the other. It became obvious that he liked forest green, burgundy, and navy blue, which revelation confirmed the info I'd gathered in Vegas. That felt like a good start. Between us, we sketched the house on an oversize piece of poster board.

Guy carried some of the figures in his head. "We had to measure all the rooms when we installed the new bathroom plumbing. Guess some of the numbers just stuck. You probably should check them all for accuracy, but they'll do to be going on with."

We had a stimulating evening. When we stopped for a tea break at ten o'clock, I got up my nerve to ask personal questions. "Guy, I may seem nosy but I think it's only fair that we exchange some information. I'm thirty-three years old, single, have never married, plus I own my business and this house. My parents are living and I have an older brother, who has a wife and three small boys. That makes me an aunt. What about you?"

Guy drained his teacup and gave me a grin. "How interesting. Well, to begin with, I'm definitely not an aunt and I rather doubt I'll ever achieve uncle status. I'm thirty-six years old and single. Never been married either, although Mother would like to see me with a wife and a flock of children. I have a younger brother named Ransome. He's divorced and a bit of a playboy."

"Tell me, Guy, what's your mother like? Will I see much of her?"

"You possibly may. She's interested in the house because she sees it as our future family seat. Our home in Scotland is an old stone heap that's falling down around her ears. She'd like to see me settled in Hollystone House with her living in the nearby Dower House. That could be another restoration project. Anyway don't be surprised if she shows up with Ellen, her maid, George, the footman, and Mrs. Hardcastle, the cook. Probably the first room you should tackle is one for her visits."

"Good heavens. Where will the servants stay?"

"Remember I told you the fourth floor of the house was designed for servants' quarters? The rooms are still usable. They're probably dusty and full of castoff furniture and old junk. You can hire some local women to dig in with buckets and mops."

"Where would I stay? Perhaps I should write 'fix up a room on the fourth floor for myself' as the first item on my to-do list."

"That should be your first priority, but you can pick any room in the house for yourself. Take the master bedroom. You're going to need an office and it has an entire suite of rooms you could use for that."

When we noticed the time, it was close to two o'clock in the morning and we were both surprised. Ten hours had elapsed without either of us being aware of time passing. I had pages of notes and felt overwhelmed by the job I'd landed.

Guy called a cab and when it came, he didn't linger. But he did give me another one of those mind-bending kisses. I had the notion that we were both using the kiss as a test. Did it give us the same buzz as the first one? He made no comment, but every nerve ending in my body felt electrified.

CHAPTER 6

The next four weeks passed in a flurry of frantic activity. I finished my decorating commitments but delayed telling my parents of my upcoming move. I dug out my passport and began laying out clothes and equipment to take. Closing up my house and dealing with a myriad of details made the days fly by. The airline ticket arrived from Guy and it was for business class. Nice touch.

I kept putting off the hardest thing to do. I needed to drive out to Elmhurst and inform my parents that their wayward child would be leaving the area for the next year or two. I expected static and I received a boatload of it the evening I went to eat dinner with them.

When I told my mother on the phone that I wanted to come out and tell them something, the silly woman jumped to an erroneous conclusion. She so hoped I'd announce my impending marriage. Even an engagement with no date set would satisfy her. She kept saying, "But is it just you coming out, Glennie? You're welcome to bring a guest."

Although I assured her I'd arrive alone, when I came in the door she peered behind me to see if I'd smuggled in a fiancé.

Mother is tall, as I am, and we look somewhat alike. However her once red-hair has faded to a mix of gray and brown. I hugged her and she seemed stiff and resistant.

My heart-shaped face came from Dad. He must have been quite a catch in his youth. A stocky man, his hug warmed and comforted me.

Mother fixed an especially good dinner that evening. The prime rib and Staffordshire potatoes tasted superb. I couldn't help but think that I might not enjoy a meal this good for a long time. Mom's a wonderful cook and concentrates on keeping a spotless house. Actually she's an over organized perfectionist.

When we'd eaten enough to founder a horse, I kept them in suspense no longer. "Mom, Dad, I've signed a terrific contract." I emphasized *contract* to show them my commitment to the job and that I'd made a professional arrangement. "The owner of a stately home in England chose me to decorate the place and it's going to take between one and two years. The mansion, called Hollystone House, sits in the country outside London. Isn't that the most amazing thing? I'm really excited and it's a wonderful opportunity."

The questions came at me like a shower of arrows. Who, what, where, why, and when? Mother started gently enough. "And what is the owner's name, dear?"

"He's a Mr. Guy McLeod."

In his gruff voice Dad cut to the heart of the matter. "Is he married, Glennie?"

The questioning went on and on with the tension growing. It felt like a courtroom cross-examination except that the persons asking the questions both acted for the prosecution. I struggled to put up a good defense but it turned into a rough go.

I'll admit that at the end I cheated a bit. Since Guy wasn't married, I leaned heavily on his mother. "Mr. McLeod is a single Scottish gentleman who doesn't use his title. His mother, Lady Sheila McLeod, will be in residence to supervise my work. You see, he travels continually in his business and will be in England only on rare occasions." Little did I know how true that would be and how rarely I'd see him.

Mother decided to attack from a different direction. "You can't just close up your house and leave it for all that time."

Dad followed her right up. "You can't leave your business for a year or two and then expect to come back to it."

"You're a little too late with those arguments. I've fulfilled all my decorating commitments. In four days a lineman is coming to disconnect the phone and my house is essentially shutdown and prepared for my absence. Michael will look after it, check it in the winter, and hire someone for lawn care. It's over. My life in Oakbrook, Illinois, is finished and I may never come back." I had no idea whether my future would include Guy McLeod but I could hope.

For forty-five minutes I sat in my parent's overstuffed living room and sweated out the grilling Mom and Dad put me through. When I'd taken all I could bear, I stood to leave. "I can close my house, I can leave my business, and I'm going to do it. Henry Bruce drew up a contract for me and it's signed and sealed. This is an opportunity that may never come my way again and I'm grabbing it with both hands. You may not like or approve of my actions, but it's a done deal. I have a plane ticket, I've already shipped a batch of luggage by air freight, and I leave in four days."

"Why didn't you tell us sooner, Glennie?"

"Because I knew you'd give me a hard time and I wasn't sure I had the strength for the battle."

"But we're just concerned with your safety and well being." Dad spoke in his rumbling, bass voice and tears started in my eyes. I would miss him.

"I know you are, but the time has come for me to cut loose the umbilical cord and become an adult in your eyes. If you could only be pleased for me and wish me well, I'd be so happy. Can you do that?"

Mom kept right on in a tight, quavery voice. "But you don't know this man. What if he doesn't pay you? What if he makes advances toward you? You simply can't do this foolish thing."

I looked around the room that I would never feel at home in again. How had our family deteriorated to this level of suspicion and distrust? At least I felt lucky enough to have memories of a great childhood. The arrival of the dreaded puberty changed our family drastically.

I grabbed my jacket and purse and headed for the door. I'd almost made it to the porch when I stuck my head back inside. "It hurts me a lot that you don't credit me with good business sense or think I can look after myself. How foolish of me to think you'd be pleased. I'll send you my address after I'm settled. Good bye."

I drove home clutching the steering wheel in anger and frustration. When I walked in the door of my house, I grabbed the ringing phone. I knew it would be Mother. "Glennie, you must listen to us. You don't have the experience to deal with a man like this English fellow. He'll cheat you or seduce you; you wait and see."

I cut her off. "Goodbye, Mother," and hung up the phone with a bang. I would not take any more of this you're-our-little-girl guff. I'd finished with letting them treat me like an airhead. I've fought for everything I ever wanted and if the folks continued to nag and hound me, I would stay as far away from them as possible.

When I announced that I wanted to become a decorator the roof caved in. Mother had an immediate opinion with which to beat me about the ears. "Decorators are unstable people. Some of them have questionable a-ah, unsavory sexual habits. No daughter of mine is going into a profession as unsuitable as interior design."

In this one instance Dad stood up for me. He offered to finance my years at design school but he added a rider. "You'll have to go to school in the Chicago area. You're too young to rush off to California to that Parson's School of Design you mentioned. We want you nearby so we can keep an eye on you." I'd learned how to compromise and considered winning half the battle a pretty good deal.

Over the next four days I let the answering machine screen my phone calls. I refused to speak to my parents and did not return the plaintive messages Mother left.

I did have a satisfying farewell dinner with my brother and his wife. Sarah is a great cook and we sat down to an all-American meal of ribs, hash-brown casserole, and broccoli salad. Over raspberry pie, Michael had a few questions. "How long do you expect to be gone, Glennie?"

"After the hell the folks have put me through the last few days, I may never come back. What happened to our folks, Michael? I don't think they've always been so obsessed with controlling me."

"It's hard to figure. Sometimes I think Dad is slipping a little. At work he's often preoccupied. The grab for control may be a symptom of the worry that age is going to take away their power over their lives. And as part of that, their power over us."

"Well, it's a mess, whatever the reason. I'm fed up and can't wait to flee the country."

Sarah cleverly changed the subject. "Tell us about the man you're going to work for, Glennie. You said he was single. Does that mean you might have a romantic interest in him?"

"I wish I knew. Maybe. He's charming and very attractive but his lifestyle doesn't lend itself to a stable relationship. He travels constantly. It's a big deal that he's promised to meet me when I arrive. I can't help wondering why he wants to fix up this big old house. If he doesn't change his habits, he'll never live there."

Michael forked up his last bite of pie. "It's an unusual situation, but we wish you the best and hope it works out. I'll look after your place and listen, if you get into any kind of an iffy situation and need money or rescuing, call me."

"You are a pal, brother."

When I left that evening my nephews—Huey, Dewey and Louie—no wait, that's Jared, Mickey, and Tom, all gave me huge, sticky hugs. I knew I'd miss them—their grins, and their small, wiggly bodies.

On the way home I let a few tears slide down my cheeks. I do love Michael and his family. When would I see them again?

The one person who truly shared my excitement was Moira Fitzgerald, my friend from design school. "Glennie, it's the chance of a lifetime. Oh, I wish I were the one going. But I shouldn't be jealous of your good fortune. You're one lucky girl. Can I fly over and visit you at your manor house?"

"You know I'd welcome you with open arms. You could probably give me some good advice on how to tackle the job. It's a huge barn of a place."

"You don't need me for decorating ideas. You'll do a super job. Do you think this fellow has any real interest in you?"

"Everyone asks me that. I don't know. I hope so. He's very attractive and I could be interested. I think it's fair to say we'll check out our reactions to each other."

"Lucky girl!"

"I know I'm lucky. This move is a door opening on the rest of my life. Maybe I'll come back here and maybe I'll settle in England. I'm going to go do the job and let life happen to me."

CHAPTER 7

As the plane took off from O'Hare Airport I mentally reviewed the list of things I'd packed for England. A couple of weeks ago I'd shipped two enormous boxes. One contained every fabric sample I could lay my hands on. The other had notes, reference books, hand tools, and the large cardboard layout of Hollystone House.

My personal luggage weighed seventy pounds over the limit but I happily paid the excess charge. I needed decent clothes for all seasons, plus paint-covered jeans for work. I couldn't do the job without my computer disks, scissors, and all the gadgets I wanted at my fingertips. I'd buy a new computer in London as mine wouldn't work with the British electrical system. I worried whether my disks would function over there but no one seemed to know. There must be computer wizards in England.

It seemed like a treat to settle into my comfortable business-class seat. I'd never want to travel coach again. How relaxing to order a glass of wine from the flight attendant. The frantic weeks before my departure exhausted me. After working eighteen hours a day and getting five hours sleep at night, as had happened the last few days, I simply fall apart.

My seatmate turned out to be large, overly talkative woman. I listened with half my mind while the other half kept thinking about Guy. After sipping my drink, I tuned out Mrs. Blabbermouth and fell into a deep sleep. I woke only when the flight attendant served a light breakfast. I'd needed some catch-up time and it felt great to wake up bright-eyed and bushy-tailed, as Grandma James used to say. Now I couldn't wait to start on Guy McLeod's house.

When we began our descent into Heathrow Airport I thought about Guy with growing excitement. He'd promised to meet me at the airport and I assumed he'd be a man of his word. My seatmate seemed in no hurry to deplane and I brewed up a case of the jitters before she finally stood and began to rummage in the overhead bin. What if Guy thought I wasn't on the plane and left.

After moving into the aisle toward the exit, I rushed down the ramp, loaded with my carry-on luggage. I scanned the crowd for a tall, blond man. He would tower above most of the people waiting. It seemed impossible that I could miss him even in that huge barn of a terminal.

When I saw no sign of him, my heart plummeted below my belt. My euphoria melted away and chilly apprehension replaced it. Maybe I'd looked in the wrong direction so I swiveled my eyes the other way. While I walked toward baggage claim, I scanned the crowd from side to side. Where could he be? I hovered on the verge of panic. If he didn't show, that left me on my own in a foreign land. I had no idea how to get to Upper Halsey or Hollystone House. Maybe I should find a call box and try to phone Guy. He gave me three numbers when he came to Chicago. Surely he'd answer one of them.

In the baggage claim area I spotted a bank of phones and headed toward them. I'd try Guy's cell number first. Maybe he went to some other part of the airport or got held up in traffic. Any number of things could keep him from showing up at Heathrow on time. I could have him paged in the airport too. Those possibilities gave me plenty of options and I felt less frightened. But still I had a clutch in my gut, a feeling of abandonment.

I dug in my purse to find the phone numbers and stiffened my shoulders. Could this be a gigantic hoax? What if Guy McLeod was only fooling with me and had no stately house to decorate. God forbid that my mother called it right with her misgivings. I felt a large, icy stone, surrounded by bumblebees, in my stomach. I hung onto my ragged nerves with all my might.

With no warning, someone tapped me on the shoulder. I jumped and whirled around with a start, expecting to see Guy. A man moved backward to avoid my stepping on him. He smiled and held out his hand. "Glenna James?" I nodded and took his hand. It felt warm and welcoming. "I'm John Fordyce. My cousin, Guy McLeod, sent me to meet you. He got himself detained in Kuwait and hopes to return in a few days."

"Oh, thank heavens he sent you." The words tumbled out and I dropped my open purse. I flushed red with embarrassment as John and I scrabbled around on the floor, picking up Kleenex, lipstick, and a tin of Altoids. "I thought I'd been stood up and left hanging. I wasn't sure what to do."

This John Fordyce had a deep, musical voice and exuded a strong sense of competence. He looked entirely different from Guy. I never would have guessed they were cousins. His brown hair curled all over his head and he wasn't nearly as tall. Maybe 5-foot-10-or-11. I immediately relaxed. I felt assured that he'd look after me. I have no clue why my nerves were so on edge. I've looked after myself for years without help. Maybe my folks' harping had finally gotten to me.

"Miss James, I'll grab a luggage trolley and we'll collect your cases. Please show me which ones to snatch off the belt."

He came back with a rattling cart and I pointed to my bags. "There, that olive-green suitcase. See it has houses painted on the side."

"Very clever of you, miss. Is that similar bag yours also?"

"Oh, yes. And snag that black tin trunk covered with flowers."

As he loaded the bags, he glanced up at me. "Did you paint them yourself?"

"Yes, I did. What do you think?"

"I think you're quite a clever lassie and Guy was brilliant to hire you to do up his house." This jolly fellow beamed a smile on me and any fears I had left melted away.

John Fordyce trundled the cart along the large hallway. He led me through passport control and customs with no hitches. I relaxed completely when I realized that he was making all this easy for me. We left the airport building, flung my bags on a shuttle van, and leaped on ourselves.

The little bus took us to the car parks. Out in a far corner we exited the van and John led me to a dusty, red Land Rover. Of course, that was the lorry. He heaved my bags in the pickup box with ease. He opened the passenger door for me and I grasped the warm, firm hand he held out. The step stood high off the ground and he boosted me into the seat.

In minutes we merged with the multitude of vehicles on the M-25, the main artery circling London. I knew there wasn't a possibility I'd be able to plunge into traffic like that where everyone drove on the wrong side of the motorway.

I quickly lost track of where we were, so I turned to study the fellow who drove me to my future. Hustling after him in the airport, I'd noted he had a trim build and broad shoulders. He certainly managed my luggage with ease. Now I could see he had an open, attractive face with a charming smile. He glanced at me occasionally with his warm, brown eyes.

John concentrated on his driving until we turned onto a side road where the traffic lessened considerably. Then he looked at me. "Well, Miss Glenna, I hope you aren't too upset that Guy didn't meet you. He said I should treat you with great care and explain about his detainment in that heathen, oil country. He told me that if he left in time to meet you, he'd lose a large contract. He probably wouldn't be able to pay the bills for Hollystone House without it. I hope you aren't too angry with him."

"No, I understand. Business is important. That's why I'm here. I'm a businessperson who decorates homes to earn my living. Tell me how you knew who I was. How did you pick me out of that huge crush of people?"

"Guy said you were a tall, slender, young woman with gorgeous, red hair, brilliant green eyes, and a lovely fair complexion. How could I miss? You were the only one who fit that description."

My fair complexion blushed crimson, but I bravely went on with my questions. "Where do you fit into the scheme of things? Guy never mentioned you."

"Ach, that's so like him. He's frightfully forgetful at times. Comes from having too much on his mind. I'm a cross between a personal secretary, an investment counselor, and a butler. I do all the jobs no one else does. If the daily maid goes home at night and leaves the dirty dishes, I wash them. If Guy wants important papers removed from the safe and faxed to him, I do that too. When it's tax time, I figure what Guy owes and send a check to the Inland Revenue. My job now is to assist you. I'm to drive you where you want to go and move or carry heavy things. He suggested that I should trap mice and kill spiders as well. I'll help you engage workmen, make you cups of tea, and type whatever correspondence you require."

"My word! I can't imagine how I ever did a job without you at my elbow."

John beamed a smile my way and ducked his head. "We're driving through the village of Upper Halsey. There's the kirk or church. Across the street you'll see the butcher and next is the food shop. I'll do the marketing for you and I can fix simple meals."

I tried to take it all in, the town, the shops, and all the help John would provide.

We left the village and drove north into a wooded rural area. He lifted his arm and pointed to the left. "Look over to the west. You'll see Hollystone any minute now."

A wall of reddish stone came into view beside the narrow road. From one end to the other espaliered holly bushes nestled against it. I brilliantly deduced that the name of the estate came from them. We drove through a black wrought-iron gate that stood open, and followed an asphalt road for about a half-mile. Oak and beech trees, lined the drive. We paused in front of a grand building of the same rusty-red stone as the walls. This was Hollystone House and its beauty took my breath away. The gray slate roof, the turrets, and the towers created a fairy-tale castle. Those wonderful Holly bushes surrounded the house and gave it a grounded aspect.

I shot a glance at John Fordyce. "I never dreamed Hollystone House would be such a handsome building. I must be the luckiest decorator in the world. I'm scared to death I'm not good enough to do the job. This house is the challenge of a lifetime."

"Don't fret, Miss Glenna. All you have to do is work on one room at a time. You'll do a grand job. Guy wouldn't have engaged you if he had any doubts about your ability. Now let's go inside. I'm ready for a cup of tea and I don't doubt you are too."

"Oh, yes. Tea sounds wonderful. How did you know I was a tea drinker?"

"Guy faxed me all of your particulars."

"That's interesting. He remembers some things but is very forgetful about other details. Like telling me I would have a very talented helper. Were you going to be here anyway or was Guy's absence the only reason you came?"

"I intended to come in a few days after Guy had you settled. I guess he planned to break it to you gently that you wouldn't be here all alone."

I mulled that over for a minute, but as we mounted wide stone steps all my attention turned to the house. John unlocked the front door and we stepped into an enormous hall with a vaulted ceiling. The chamber, paneled in oak stained dark from centuries of wood smoke, appeared wonderfully appealing. We walked ahead and I looked with awe at the magnificent staircase. A fireplace filled the far wall. This must be the original part of the house, the great hall. My mind took off like a butterfly and flitted from idea to idea. Oh my, what I could do with this space.

I turned to my new assistant. "Can we defer the tea? I want so much to see at least some of the house. Please give me a tour."

"I'll gladly lead you to some of the rooms, miss. Follow me. On the right side of the hall you'll find the lounge or parlor." He opened a set of carved oak doors. What a big room! I thought about the vast amount of furniture it would require to fill the space. How many sofas, end tables, and lamps would I need to buy?

"On the left through those doors is the library. The original bookcases were spoiled from damp rot so you'll need to replace them. The books are boxed in the attic. Behind the stairway is the dining room and next to it lies the butler's pantry. You'll need to order china, crystal glassware, and silverware for the dinners I'm sure Guy will plan in the future."

"I will? Isn't there any silver or dishes?"

"Lady McLeod has the family treasures in Scotland. Nothing came with the house that we know about. I've collected some odds and ends of things for us to use until the good pieces can be purchased."

"Mr. Fordyce, where is the kitchen?"

"Ach, surely you know how these old piles of stone were built. We're on the first floor and there is a ground floor below us. The kitchen is there along with the storerooms and the estate office. And please call me John. I don't think we need to be so formal when it's just the two of us working here."

"Right, and I'm Glenna. What happens in the estate office?"

"I'll be keeping the household books there, as well as dealing with Guy's finances. It all goes into the computer. It's my hidey-hole where I can go when I need to figure the laird's taxes or take care of other business for him. Are you going to need a place for an office?"

"I'll need some kind of a workroom. What do you suggest?"

"Beyond the library sits the morning room where the original family had breakfast and lunch." He opened a door to show me.

"It's a nice room but I'll need a really big table to spread out samples and plans."

"Then, Miss Glenna, I suggest you move into the dining room. There's a large table in there and I'll get you some file cabinets at the local auction. How will that be?"

John opened a door beyond the stairway and I peered over his shoulder. "It's a terrific room. Now what about that tea? Can we have it in the morning room? It's so sunny and pleasant."

"I'll be right back with some lunch."

I sat at a small, folding table and tried to sort through what John had shown me of the house. To say I was overwhelmed is an understatement. I'd not envisioned buying china and dinnerware. Probably the kitchen would need cookware and I wondered about small appliances. I would have to check the cupboards for equipment or at least ask John.

It occurred to me that all those bedrooms, which I hadn't seen yet, would require linens. Bedspreads and draperies had been on my list, but sheets and towels would also be needed. It sounded as if this house lacked just about everything.

Mr. Fordyce, er — John sprinted up the back stairs from the ground floor with the tea. He balanced a tray, holding a brown earthenware pot and chunky mugs, on his shoulder and carried a plate of rare roast beef sandwiches. He placed the food on the table and pulled a packet of shortbread cookies from his pocket. We were both hungry and deferred discussing our project until after we ate. We made away with most of the food and I started to feel energized about the project ahead.

"Do you do the cooking, John, or am I expected to take my turn in the kitchen?"

"I'm not a bad cook, but you may be much better at it. I rather hoped we'd share the duties. We can set up a schedule or whoever is the least busy can do the catering. What do you think?"

"I'm sort of mediocre in the kitchen. I won't starve you but I don't seem to have the imagination a good cook needs. Why don't we start with the least busy person preparing the meals? If it doesn't work, then we can make other arrangements."

I began to think that working with John Fordyce looked like a plus and from the twinkle in his eye, might even be fun. I found I liked him and his easy manner. He was polite but comfortable to be around. He treated me like a real person. His attitude made me feel confident and at ease with him and my job.

CHAPTER 8

At the end of my first two weeks at Hollystone House, I managed to tour every room and verify its dimensions. John and I crawled around on our hands and knees, stretching the big tape measure between us. "All right, Miss Glenna, I make that out to be twelve feet and six inches."

"John, call me Glenna. You said twelve-foot-six, right? If I'd known we'd spend so much time on the floor I'd have brought kneepads with me. Let's try that one again, standing up."

We pulled the tape across the same room. "That comes out to twelve feet, two and one half inches."

"Oh, darn it! We'll have to keep measuring on the floor. It's important that we get the carpet the right size or the pieces will never fit. I suppose a place this old has sagged and shrunk in places."

"Maybe it's time for a tea break, Miss — -ah — Glenna."

"I'm ready. If you'll brew the tea, I'll get the dimensions of the windows in this room. See you in the morning room in ten minutes."

"Righto."

John's tray contained a plate of flaky-looking rolls or buns. He also had clotted cream and raspberry jam. "These biscuits are delicious. Where did you get them? You didn't whip them up yourself, did you?"

"Biscuits are those flat sweet cakes you call cookies. These are scones. They're an old Scottish favorite and our nanny raised me on them." Then he smiled and gave me a wink. "They sell all sorts of treats in the village bake shop."

The house consisted of the central block with wings off to the right and left. On the first floor the right wing contained the master bedroom, a vast bathroom complete with Jacuzzi, a sitting room, and a study. The closet was the size of a bedroom, which it probably served as before the present remodeling.

Later John explained the layout to me. "The closet may be a holdover from the old days when the master of the house had a dressing room, usually with a single bed in it. He could spend the night there if he was in his cups or if the lady of the manor felt delicate."

"What a good idea. Most of today's homes don't run to such amenities."

Going upward to the second floor wings, I explored the new bathrooms and closets and poked my nose into all the bedrooms. I discovered the combination sewing and linen room. I planned to buy a sewing machine to put in there so I could run up little pieces of trim myself rather than bother with a seamstress.

The third floor contained the expected bedrooms, baths, and closets, plus a large sitting room, which could be added to a bedroom to form a suite. The children's classroom and night nursery would make another wonderful suite.

Guy's room count must have been an estimate. As I carefully listed twenty bedrooms, I reworked my notes on the colors and fabrics each would require. It seemed like a daunting challenge as I matched prints with solids to make a coordinated scheme for each room.

John came with me to explore the fourth floor. "The rooms up here are like wee cupboards. Nasty little cubicles for the servants, of which I am one." He opened a door and I could see what he meant. I walked on down the hall and pushed open another door. The room contained a narrow bed, a dresser with a drawer stuck half-open, and a twelve-by-twelve-inch closet. The closet had no door and was full of men's clothes.

"Oh, this is your room, isn't it, John? I'm sorry I barged right in."

"No harm done. I'm camping out for the time being. Once you finish a room or two I'll move down a floor and be more comfortable. You really should know where I'm staying in case the ghost walks one night and you need to find me."

"Ghost! What ghost?"

"Oh, all self-respecting ancient houses have their own live-in ghost. Ours is Lady Minerva Paget. The history of the house says that she died giving birth to her thirteenth child in October of 1763. Local lore has it that she became quite disenchanted with her husband, his lordship, and proceeded to haunt him after he brought home a second wife."

"How exciting. Does she show herself or make clanking noises?"

"I've heard nothing so far, but there are rumors that she groans or weeps as if her heart was broken. If she materializes for you, be sure and tell me, Miss Glenna."

"Hey, ditch the 'miss.' If I'm to call you John, you can certainly call me Glenna."

"Of course I can. You're more informal in the States than we are. Frankly, I think this country could do with a bit of unbending."

On the day I arrived John showed me to my room on the second floor, above the hall. It delighted me that it was a turret chamber with tall narrow windows. The furnishings were plain but the dresser drawers closed and the closet held most of my clothes and luggage. What a wonderful place to retire after a hard day of work.

A few weeks after I settled into my room, I found John down in his office. "Is there an extra chair somewhere in this house? I really would like to have one in my room. Since I have those windows I'd enjoy looking out over the fields and meadows."

"Follow me, ma'am, and you can have all the chairs you want." We hiked to the fourth floor, north wing and from there to an attic. There behind a locked door waited a marvelous collection of antique furniture. I've no idea why we left this area unexplored on our earlier excursions through the house.

I stood in the doorway with my hands on my hips. "There's wonderful stuff up here. Can't we use it to furnish the house?"

John peered over my shoulder. "A few pieces are okay but some of the larger items are water damaged and need to be refinished. Can you do that?"

44

"I can but I'd rather find someone else to do the work. It's not hard but I won't have time to do it all myself. We're going to need painters and people who wallpaper too. Do you know where we'll be able to get some help?"

"Whenever you're ready I'll go to the labor exchange in the village. People queue up there looking for jobs and wait till someone hires them. How soon are you going to need someone?"

"Soon. Real soon. Like Monday. I'm going to decide on paint colors by tomorrow and get the order to the shop. Look at this neat chair. It's a rocker and the finish on it is beautiful. Can you carry it down to my room?"

John easily hefted the chair and I trailed after him down the handsome oak staircase. While he placed the chair in my room I tore on down to the dining room where I'd spread my supplies. I grabbed a pen and yellow pad and trotted up to the fourth floor again. Much more of this chasing up and down and I'd be slimmer than nature made me. Of course at the rate I gobbled up scones, I might not be losing any weight.

Tablet in hand, I inventoried and listed the condition of the furniture. Out of eighty-one pieces, about forty needed some repair, varnish, or at least polishing. John could engage the extra help right away.

In the midst of our busy days I didn't think much about Guy but at night I'd crawl into bed and realize that he hadn't called me. Not once!

CHAPTER 9

After a couple of weeks, Guy McLeod finally did call me. When he didn't meet me at the airport I shoved him to the back of my mind and forgot about him. He apologized prettily for not showing up at the airport. "So how's the work going? How many rooms are finished?"

"Don't joke, Guy. This is serious business to me. No rooms are finished. We've made a decent start and I'm happy about that. John hired a delightful young couple, Jilly and Harry Burns. They'll alternate between painting and refinishing furniture. While the coats of varnish dry, I'll start them on the walls. Harry is artistic and innovative. He's a real find. We're letting them camp up on the fourth floor. I think they were down to their last five pounds when John brought them home."

"Well, I hope you're going to pay them a living wage."

"They receive a modest salary and we feed them three times a day. Harry looks to be eight feet tall and he can't weigh over a hundred twenty-five pounds. Jilly is beautiful. She has dark-olive skin, with big brown eyes, and black wavy hair. I swear she's a displaced Ethiopian princess. Why don't you come home and meet them?"

"Okay, how about tomorrow? Is that soon enough?"

"Tomorrow it is. Shall we expect you for lunch, tea, or dinner?"

"Dinner will be fine. Since I'll wing in from Argentina, I truly doubt I can be there before six o'clock."

The minute I hung up the phone I ran to find John. I tracked him down in the kitchen assembling the tea tray. I helped carry things up to the morning room. While we made a meal out of scones with clotted cream and plum jam, I told him and the Burnses the news.

"Mr. Guy is coming home tomorrow night. We need to spend the next twenty-four hours completing all of our half-done jobs so it will look as if we've been hard at work during his absence. Also it would be awfully nice if we had a really super dinner for him. Who wants to cook?"

Jilly, who up to this point had barely said a word to any of us, piped up. "If you please, Miss Glenna, I could roast a joint of beef with vegetables."

"Great. Talk to John about what you'll want in the way of groceries. I can make a trifle for dessert. Is there any sherry left, John? I think I used most of it for last Sunday's sweet."

He stood up, looking like a man with a purpose. "Sounds good. I'll fix some tidbits or other for a starter, buy sherry for your dessert, and get a good red wine to have with dinner. In fact, first thing tomorrow morning I'll go to the shops. Now what do you want completed before Guy's arrival?"

"Since we'll have to eat in here I'd like to have this room finished. Harry, it looks as if you have all the green paint on the walls. They look wonderful to me."

"Yes, ma'am, I do. You can see I've made a start on the murals. I'll finish the white latticework design by tonight and add the vines and flowers tomorrow. And I forgot to tell you that I found a large wrought-iron table in the basement storerooms. It's round and will seat about twelve people. And there are six matching chairs. It will be much better than this bitty folding table we use now. I used up some forest-green paint on the chairs earlier this week so they should be dry enough to sit on by tomorrow evening."

"Harry, that's wonderful. But we have to have curtains and a tablecloth. I'll go to the shops and see what I can find in the morning. Can I catch a ride with you, John, when you go for the groceries?"

"Certainly, you may. I'll leave at 9:00 a.m. Be ready. But what can we do about the master bedroom? Will we be able to have it ready for our master?" he asked with a twinkle in his eye.

"Right after dinner we'll go to the furniture storeroom and pick out pieces that are in good shape. I'll buy sheets and some sort of curtains, but I hate to spend money for a bedspread we may not be able to use later."

John's face lit up. "I forgot to tell you something, Miss Glenna. In the attics there are trunks full of old drapes, bedding of all sorts, and even some boxes of bric-a-brac. Maybe you won't have to go to the shops tomorrow."

"John, for the very last time, ditch the 'miss.' This is the final time I'm warning you. Next time you call me 'miss', I'm going to wake up the ghost and make sure she haunts you."

"Yes, ma'am!"

When I went to bed that night I lay awake for almost an hour, excited about Guy's visit and wondering what it would be like when he came. Would he be pleased with our work? Might he be coming to see me or only to check on the house progress? I'd been so busy that I'd kept Guy in a separate compartment of my mind. I could bring him forward when I had a few minutes and fantasize about the future, but would reality be anything like my dreams?

We busted our butts the next day. Harry finished the morning room, which looked fresh and pretty with his white lattice and drifts of pink and yellow flowers. They looked like snapdragons to me. He turned a large fan on the walls to blow the murals dry and waft the paint odor outside.

Jilly gathered bouquets from the garden for the table and put a nice arrangement in Guy's bedroom. In between cooking dinner and picking flowers she managed to get a last coat of China-rose paint on the master bedroom walls. I cleaned and polished a bed, dresser, rocking chair, and campaign chest for the room after John and Harry moved the pieces down from the fourth floor. We again left the windows open to air out the paint smell.

The attic boxes overflowed with goodies. I found draperies with a burgundy and blue paisley design — twelve panels. I shook them, hung them out in the sunshine to air and later ran an iron over them. On my newly purchased sewing machine I simply stitched the panels together till I had a bedspread. Then I whipped up some pillow shams. There were old ivory sheets with lace trim, which I tossed into the washer and hung outside to bleach. Other attic finds included a box of dishes in a purple pansy pattern and a yellow tablecloth for the round table.

When Guy McLeod, driven by John in the Land Rover, came up the drive, we were as ready as we could be. I escorted him to his master suite, casually directed him to wash up in his bath, using the soft, linen towels we reclaimed from the attic. Before I turned to go back to the hall, he gave me a bear hug that almost crushed my lungs and followed it up with several kisses.

"You've done well, my dear refurbisher. This room is lovely. And those comfortable chairs in the hall look welcoming. I'll meet you there shortly for a before dinner drink."

John's tidbits tasted hot and savory. Guy met Harry and Jilly and they acted terribly pleased to be offered a glass of wine with the owner of the house. Jilly slipped away to finish dinner. When we led Guy to the morning room he stopped in surprise. "What a charming room. I don't remember it being like this. It looks like a garden."

We gave Harry artistic credit for the painting and Jilly chose that moment to come in with an enormous platter she found in the kitchen. The roast sat in the center surrounded by carrots, beets, and Brussels sprouts, with parsley scattered over all. It looked fit for a king.

Next she scampered up the steps, carrying a bowl heaped with mashed potatoes and a pitcher of gravy. We had a little trouble convincing Harry and Jilly to eat with us. They felt it was not the thing, but John and I insisted. This small corner of England had become democratic.

We spent a delightful evening. Guy regaled us with stories of his travels and the young couple listened with their mouths open. "The last time I flew to Cape Town the captain announced over the PA, 'Due to some unforeseen problems at the Cape Town airport, we won't be able to land there. Instead we'll divert to Johannesburg where you can change to a flight for Cape Town.' No one offered more explanations and we traveled another half day. The next morning I read an article in the Cape Town newspaper that someone stole the landing lights at the airport. We couldn't land because it happened to be nighttime."

Harry, who normally stayed remarkably silent, exclaimed, "Cor, I'd be afraid to even go up in one of them planes."

The five of us finished two bottles of red wine, which combined with our high-pressure day, left all of us sleepy. We managed to do major damage to the trifle and then John and the Burns drifted off to their rooms.

Guy helped me carry the dirty dishes and leftovers to the basement kitchen. I filled the big sink with boiling hot water and soap and dumped the dishes in to soak overnight. We put bits of leftover trifle and the roast beef into the fridge and then we slowly climbed back up to the first floor. We dropped onto the comfortable, but ugly, old sofa in front of the hall fireplace and began to talk.

"You've impressed me with what you've done so far, Glenna. What's next on your agenda?"

"There are detailed plans in the dining room, which I'm using as command central. Do you want to look at them now?"

"No, we're both too tired. I know you knocked yourself out yesterday and today, and obviously your crew of helpers did too. Get a good night's sleep and we'll have a conference in the morning. Right now just tell me generally how it's going. Do you and John work well together?"

"I truly don't think I could have made it this far without him. He's kind, he's smart, and he often reads my mind. He skipped me right over any adjustment period as far as finding the shops and getting acquainted with service people. Why didn't you tell me he'd be here to help?"

"I forgot. It frustrated me that I couldn't make it back to meet you. Also I ran out of time to call you. You'd left Chicago when the complications became apparent. I managed to reach John in Scotland and asked him to speed down here a few days early and take over. Did he get you a credit card?"

"Oh, yes. I spend your money quite freely these days. We've ordered one hundred and fifty gallons of paint or emulsion, as you call it, and we have an expedition to Harrods planned for a furniture spree. I'm glad you're here to approve that. Also, do you realize we must buy linens? All the beds need sheets. The ones I found in the attic to put on your bed are so worn that you'll shove a foot through one any night now. Every bed will need a spread and blankets. I plan to order American towels. I much prefer them to what I've seen here. In the morning I'll show you my lists and estimated costs. I waited for you to come before I ordered the furnishings we need. I brought a number of catalogs with me from the States and I'm ready to place orders for a lot of items when you give the word."

"It's all right, Glenna. I trust you to buy sensibly. Go ahead on the linens and furniture." With those words he moved closer and slid his long, muscular arms around me. How did he know what I needed? He felt so warm as we cuddled there, exchanging kisses. Strength flowed from his body to mine and I decided what I missed in my life was someone to love. I felt as if my daydreams would start to come true any moment now.

CHAPTER 10

The next morning I came down from my room to find John and Guy in the morning room huddled over tea and buns. John must have been out early to the bakeshop. I slipped into a chair and poured myself a cup of tea. I still felt sleepy and needed that jolt of English Breakfast to get me going.

It sounded as if the men were discussing finance and I gathered our project was solvent. So far I'd received a paycheck from John each week and I carefully banked it at the Sovereign Bank in Chartwell, a nearby town. I had no expenses while I lived at Hollystone House. John bought all the food, petrol, and everything else we needed. He seemed to be advising Guy on an investment.

Guy pointed to some papers on the table. "If you think I should sell the manufacturing mutual funds and move to computer stocks, I'll do it."

"From my research I do think it's a wise move. I've already transferred some of my investments along those lines."

The two men took notice of me at last and wished me a jolly good morning. I responded and then asked Guy how long he'd be with us.

"I have a plane out of Gatwick at 8:30 tomorrow evening. Can we take our tea and buns to your office so you can give me a report on the plans?"

"Anytime. I'm at your disposal."

"Then let's do it. I must make the most of my time while I'm here."

In the dining room I'd opened the table to its full size with all the leaves in place. After I knew about Guy's arrival I found a few minutes the day before to draft a more professional layout of the house. Well actually it took several hours, which cut severely into my bed time. First I made a scale drawing showing all five floors. Then I titled or numbered the rooms. For each room I'd assembled a numbered pile of swatches that filled the remainder of the table.

"See, Guy. Let's take the master bedroom. Here are the dimensions on the plan and this pile of samples is marked for that suite. China rose is the room color and Jilly has finished painting the walls. The carpet will be burgundy with a floral design in forest green and light shades of rose. The spread, draperies, and pillow shams will be ivory damask with a stenciled border that will match the design in the carpet. There will be two easy chairs covered by this green-and-ivory stripe and a round table with a matching green cloth. See how it works?"

"I do and I'm impressed. However, I thought the master suite was done."

"Oh no, we raided the attic for the material in there. Those old draperies won't survive cleaning. They'll fall apart at the first hint of soap and water. We just put your room together for the time you're here. What we did isn't permanent."

"I'm amazed at your ingenuity. What about the rest of the rooms adjoining the master suite?"

"This dark green tile is for the bathroom walls. We'll inset ivory tiles with rose flowers at random. You'll have thick and thirsty rose towels and rugs. Now this area is your private sitting room and the next one will be your study. We'll use the striped material on some of the sofas and chairs, but we'll combine the fabric with blue to avoid too much sameness. The carpet and window swags will be in this medium-blue shade. We'll find a desk for your study and some bookshelves and file cabinets. The walls are to be painted in very pale green and we'll stencil a border using the same pattern as in the bedroom. What do you think?"

"I like it. And all these other heaps of material are for the rest of the rooms?"

"There's a pile for each room. We won't spend so much money on the rest of the rooms. They'll be nice but we'll buy less expensive linens and furniture. John discovered a cache of antique furniture in the fourth-floor wing. Harry and Jilly are working up there refinishing pieces as fast as they can."

"Tell me about them. Where did you find them?"

"John brought them home from the labor exchange. They were down on their luck and hungry. Our plan is to fatten them up and encourage them to save their wages. Harry is artistic and a real treasure. Last evening Jilly showed us she can cook like a dream and she spent half of yesterday painting the walls in your bedroom. I'll have to say she's a jewel."

"You have quite a team here and everyone seems able to do everything. I'm truly impressed, Glenna."

"I love to work with young people. They aren't as set in their ways as older folks often are. We're going to need more help soon but right now we're doing fine."

"Glenna, I have an idea. Let's go to town later today. I'll take you to Harrods and help pick out furniture. What do you say? We could see a show tonight. I have a little apartment there where we can stay. Let's do it."

"It sounds heavenly, Guy. I'm ready for a break. What time should I be ready?"

"Let's ask John to drive us to the station about three thirty and we'll catch the three forty-five train. Pack a dress for the theater. I'll call now and see about tickets. Have you seen, *Cats?*"

"No, and I'd love to. I'll be packed and waiting. I'll spend the rest of the morning completing my lists and be ready to hit the stores."

At lunch that day we ate Jilly's tuna salad sandwiches and Guy reported on our upcoming trip to London. I categorized my lists and packed my russet silk dress. I laid out a dressy pantsuit for the train trip and to wear shopping. I wondered if John felt left out as he and I had planned to go to the city on a buying spree in a couple of weeks. Well, Guy was the boss, so I told myself it wasn't my business to worry about John.

The trip delighted me and I wanted to bounce up and down on my seat as we rode the train into the city. Guy asked me, "Are you missing your home and family?"

"Gosh, no. First of all you may not know about my family. All they

54

want to do is marry me off to some man who will 'take care of me.' They staged a huge scene when I told them about coming over here. We parted on less than cordial terms. I'm so glad to get away from frequent grillings about my love life and how I can't do anything right because I'm a girl."

"You seem amazingly competent to me, Glenna. It's hard to believe your parents wouldn't recognize your talents."

"Well, they don't, but I'm used to being treated like a child. Let's not talk about my family anymore. Tell me about the show we're going to see."

"*Cats* has run in London for years and years although I hear it's about to close. It's a rather different show in that there isn't a real story line. Just scenes put on by various cats gathered for a ball. It's the music that makes me want to see and hear it again. You'll recognize a lot of the songs."

We went to the early evening performance of Lloyd Webber's show. I loved those cats and the songs they sang, especially Grizabella and "Memories." I walked out of the theater humming the tune. We enjoyed a late dinner in a swanky restaurant and I carefully limited myself to two glasses of wine. We moved on to dance in a noisy club and when we returned to Guy's mini-flat, the clock had slipped well past the witching hour.

"How about a nightcap?" Guy turned to me with a decanter in his hand. When I turned it down, we sat close on the sofa and he placed small kisses on my elbows and on my neck, and worked his way to my lips. I began to feel so warm, hot really. My dress felt too tight and I unbuttoned the neck and cuff buttons. Guy whispered to me with his lips against my cheek. "Glennie, I'd give a lot to make love to you tonight. How would you feel about that?"

I hesitated, but knew in my heart that I didn't want to turn him down. I answered indirectly by moving closer to him and offered him my lips. He skillfully pulled me up from the sofa and led me into the main bedroom. There was another tiny bedroom where I probably should have spent the night. As he began to unbutton his shirt, I grabbed my green satin robe and dashed into the bathroom. The robe is short and full, and if I avoid bending over, it covers most of me.

I shyly stepped out of the bathroom and walked to the bed. I turned the covers down and slid between the sheets. Guy shed his clothes and joined me. He turned on his side and reached for me. "Come here, Glennie. Let me slip my arm behind you." Then he bent his head and the serious kisses began. Before long the short robe sailed over the side onto the floor. Guy treated me gently and I thought him to be quite skillful. He seemed to sense that my past experience was rather limited and I willingly allowed him to teach me.

Afterward he fell into a deep sleep and I lay beside him and replayed the entire scene in my head. Had I seemed gauche and inexperienced? Guy made certain I enjoyed pleasure along with him. Did that make him a gentleman or just a clever fellow?

Before I fell asleep, I felt a bit of regret. The experience was technically perfect but did something personal seem to be missing?

In the morning we both were sleeping hard when a maid knocked at the door with morning tea and Danish. It embarrassed me that she found us so undressed, but Guy seemed to take it in stride.

We dressed quickly and taxied to the Knightsbridge area to begin our great shopping spree. We arranged the delivery of our purchases for whenever I called for them. After we spent 50,000 pounds in Harrods alone, Guy negotiated a discount because we'd purchased so much. I was aghast at the amount of money we spent, but the dough belonged to him, not me.

As we took a cab to Euston train station, I began to cross items off my lists: three brass bedsteads, two made of delicate white-painted iron, and two complete white-and-gold French provincial bedroom suites. For the drawing room I chose two sofas of ivory damask with tiny gold plumes woven into the fabric, four wingback chairs striped in ivory and gold, and a clutch of marble-topped tables.

We'd need more furniture to fill the parlor but there were likely some usable pieces in the attic. The window treatment fabric matched that used for the sofas. I ordered ivory sheers to hang underneath the draperies. The carpet would be dark gold and Harry and I had planned a tone-on-tone paint job, ivory over wheat with just a hint of metallic gold. I grabbed some burgundy pillows with elegant gold fringe to throw in a bit of excitement and punch up the room. Modern decorators can't say three sentences with using the word punch at least once.

For the library we ordered bookshelves of walnut wood, enough to line three walls of the room from floor to ceiling. I handed over the library dimensions and a drawing indicating location of the windows and fireplace. The units would be custom-made and available in sixty to ninety days. Guy insisted on a walnut library ladder, with curved steps trimmed in brass, to reach the upper shelves. I told him, "That's an extravagance you don't need."

He said, "It's my house and there are certain things that I want to have. Do you mind?"

After his sharp words, I shut my mouth.

The spending spree went on and on. We ordered a rusty-red leather sofa and four club chairs for the library. The Burnses were refinishing a walnut library table that would help fill the room. The carpet we selected was dark brownish red with a mustard color Greek Key border.

We went wild and ordered custom draperies for the room to be made of a rich, taffeta plaid in Chinese red and eggplant with thin mustard stripes. The draperies would hang on brass rods. I immediately fell in love with the whole idea of the library.

For the dining room Harry felt we could refinish the table and after sorting through the attic treasures we found eighteen matching chairs. We purchased a handsome Ainsly china pattern called orchard gold. It came decorated with luscious fruits burnished with gold leaf. We ordered twenty-four place settings. The silver flatware had a simple design, with a touch of gold on the handle. Guy deemed crystal stemware with a gold rim a necessity.

And finally we ordered a huge Welch dresser in walnut, similar to the dining table in style and finish, to store this bounty of beautiful things. When Guy looked at a Georgian silver tea set, I put my foot down. "That can come later, Guy. We need to get to the linen department."

At the station Guy saw me settled on the train to the village, gave me a passionate goodbye kiss, and vanished into the night to find a cab to the airport. I sat in a trance for the first few minutes. Later I dug out my lists and crossed off more items. Finally I gave up and sat in the train with my shoes off and thought about the night before. One thing puzzled me. Guy was a quiet lover. No sweet nothings in my ear. I had expected more than silence.

John waited to meet me when the train arrived in Upper Halsey. I carried a whole batch of fabric swatches, plus one of those huge wallpaper sample books. I'd tucked a heap of carpet squares under my left arm. As I stepped onto the platform, I caught my heel and when I instinctively put out my hands to catch myself, bits and pieces went everywhere. While John and I crawled around, picking up the dropped items, we managed to bump heads and I dragged myself into the Land Rover with a nasty headache.

Tears ran down my cheeks as we drove to Hollystone. John parked back at the horse barns before He noticed me weeping. He swept me into his arms, struggling to pull a large, white hanky out of his pocket to mop my face. He continued to hold me tight against him. "Glennie, what's wrong? Please tell me."

I felt uncertain at first what caused my distress, besides the obvious physical things. Then it hit me. I was furious with myself that I'd gone to bed with Guy. We had an exciting time, but as I reviewed our hectic hours together, it wasn't personal. I wondered if just any girl might have fit into the day and night's activities. While nestled in John's arms, I felt a strong urge simply to stay there.

I managed to finish wiping my eyes. "I'm so sorry. My head hurts from our smashup on the train platform and I think I'm worn out. I've never shopped so intensely in my life. My feet hurt and I need to go to bed. Does your head hurt?"

"No, you must have gotten the worst of the noggin bashing. Let's go in and have a cup of tea. Then you can go to bed as soon as you like. But first I want to hear about your purchases. What did it feel like to spend money like a drunken sailor on shore leave?"

That made me laugh as I pictured Guy and me flinging pound notes to the wind. After that I began to feel better.

John had left a fire in the great hall and he carried our tea tray to a small table in front of the old sofa. We sat there and watched the flames. Then he urged me to report. "Tell me all about the shopping. What did you buy?"

"Oh, John, everything. On the train coming back I added up our purchases and the amount staggered me. Does Guy really have that kind of money?"

"Yes, he does. He didn't start out with much but he's worked hard since he left Oxford and it's piled up quite nicely. But what did you buy?"

I dug the receipts out of my purse and handed them to John. "We bought it all. There'll be a rail carload of bedspreads, pillows, sheets, and towels coming. I don't have to send to America for the towels after all. They had the thickest, softest ones possible. Harrods will need a special warehouse just to store the stuff till we're ready for it to be shipped."

He scanned the receipts one by one and then tucked them in his shirt pocket. "When are they sending your goods?"

"I'm supposed to call them when we're ready."

"I think we'd be smart to get the things here as soon as possible. Delivery is a chancy thing in this country. I'm afraid once you need certain items, you'll want them yesterday and it could take a month or more to get them here. If we order them sent now, we'll have them when we need then. Would you like for me to take care of it tomorrow?"

What a relief to have someone to share the work with. "Would you please, John? It sounds like the best thing to do. But where will we store all that stuff?"

"Some bedroom items can go into one room on the second floor and one on the third floor. We can stack the library shelves and so on here in the hall."

I interrupted him to say, "They won't be ready for a couple of months so we can worry about them later."

"Okay, scratch the shelving. The hall is big enough we may be able to put the parlor furniture in here too. If that isn't enough, the cellar is dry and there's plenty of space. We can shove boxes into the south wing off the morning room. I prefer not to have to carry a bunch of stuff up or downstairs more than once." He gave me a look. "I can see you're absolutely wiped out for tonight. You'd best be off to bed."

"The tea did me a lot of good and I feel much better. I'm sorry I wept all over your shirtfront. I don't usually do that, but we skipped lunch and I'm exhausted. In the future I'll try to refrain from such emotional displays." Later I thought I sounded quite pompous with my little apology.

"Don't worry, Glennie. You can cry on my shirtfront whenever you want."

"Thanks for the offer. I think we better make a plan for tomorrow." We organized the next day's work as we did each evening. We assigned tasks to Harry and Jilly, posting the list in the morning room. That way, whoever got up first could start right in on a job.

"The first thing for you to do, John, is be on the doorstep of the labor exchange when it opens and find us more painters, two at least. Jilly and Harry simply can't keep up with all there is to do. I'd rather be able to get the job finished in a shorter time. Then would you find someone who can install ceramic tile on the walls and floors of the master bath? While you do that, I'll post a note in each room listing the colors for the wall and the trim. Then I'll move the paint cans to the room. That way nobody can be blamed for mistakes except me. Harry and Jilly can continue to refinish the furniture upstairs." I yawned. "And now it's bed for me."

The next morning I carried a mug of tea and a plate of what was becoming my favorite breakfast, scones, to the dining room. I spent the first hour revising my swatches and room plans. In one of my rare flashes of brilliance, I decided to design the bedrooms and baths on the second floor in a more formal manner than those on the third floor. I'd use damasks, sateens, and brocades on second for coverlets and window treatments. Patchwork quilts and throw pillows would decorate the upper level. If I could lay my hands on the fabric, some Scottish tartans would look wonderful, perhaps for carpet as well.

John came back from the village with brothers, Mick and Rick Jardine. They spoke little beyond saying, "'Lo miss." They simply grabbed their equipment, hiked up stairs, and started brushing on the paint. At noon I went up to check and they had completed two walls. "Your work is very neat, fellows, I don't see a drop on the floor." But I wanted speed too. Oh, well, no one is perfect. I suppose I should settle for a good job rather than a rushed one.

Later when I met John in the kitchen I questioned him. "Who are those fellows. They don't seem like casual workers."

"They aren't. They're the local remodeling contractors. Jobs are slow right now so they eagerly came to work for us. The butcher told me about them. How does their work look?"

"They don't move too fast but I do think the walls they've completed are well-done. I've learned that one slow, thorough paint job is better than several thin coats."

John set a plate of sandwiches on the lunch tray. "And those fellows tell me they can handle the ceramic tile"

The rooms started to come together after two weeks of the brothers Jardine working away away. When Harry and Jilly completed the furniture refinishing the various woods looked beautiful. "I say, you two, you've done a super job. We'll let the furniture sit here and set up for several days before we move it. I once made a horrible mess of some tables. Tried to rearrange them before they were dry and left sticky fingerprints all over the fresh varnish. Maybe we should bring the fan up here to speed up the drying. What say you two take the rest of today off? I'll ask John to pay you and you can go enjoy yourselves. I'll even ask him if you can take the lorry."

"That would be super, Miss Glenna. We do need to pick up a few things in the shops."

CHAPTER 11

One day when I felt restless I took some time to explore outside Hollystone House. I found several barns and outbuildings. They were empty with only a wisp of hay left here and there. Behind the buildings I discovered walled gardens. Since it was early autumn, there weren't many flowers showing, just mums and asters, but it looked as if many things would come alive in the spring. As I walked farther back, I came across an orchard.

When I returned to the house my pockets and hands were full of apples. I knew how to make applesauce and that would add zest to some of our sketchy meals. It felt good to be outside. I needed to breathe fresh air and exercise more often.

No word came from Guy and I felt terrible. It was foolish of me to hop into bed with him. What did I expect? A lifelong commitment after one romantic night? As things became more hectic, I let Guy slide into the back of my mind.

Our activities heated up when a telegram arrived from his mother, Lady Sheila McLeod. It said:

PLAN TO ARRIVE 2:50 P.M. TRAIN TUESDAY STOP
ANXIOUS TO SEE HOUSE REDECORATION STOP INDEFINTE
STAY STOP ELLEN WITH ME STOP

When John read the message aloud, a nervous tension seemed to crackle through all of us. The obvious place for Lady Sheila McLeod to stay was the master suite. We had forty-eight hours to pull the project together. I called our little work force in for a conference. "All hands on deck for a massive assault on the master suite and living room. Mick and Rick, please complete grouting the bathroom tile. Harry, are you ready to finish the stencils in the study and sitting room?"

Harry nodded yes. "It won't take half a mo'."

I nodded back. "Better hop to it on the double then. John, when Harry's free, will you two start moving and uncrating furniture? The master bedroom set is in marked cartons in the hall. We'll need a bed and dresser from the fourth floor for the maid's room." We decided Lady Sheila's age and position entitled her to have the owner's rooms and if Guy showed up while his mother was in residence, he could sleep on an army cot in the basement, for all I cared.

"Jilly, let's consult on some quick and easy meals that will look as if they took hours to prepare."

"Surely, Miss Glenna. I'll start the list and check the pantry for supplies."

"Mick, do you or your brother have a wife who'd like to come help us clean this place?"

"Yes, Miss Glenna, us has got wives who'd come dust and mop for you. When do you want them?"

"How about now? You can use the phone in the library."

It took major arm-twisting but the carpet layers came at the last minute and installed yards and yards of deep gold plush in the parlor. With that complete, I hustled them into the master suite to lay the floor coverings in the bedroom and sitting room. In between ransacking the attics for whatnots and knickknacks, I frantically vacuumed fuzz and scraps off the new carpet.

Once when John and I took a minute for a cup of tea I questioned him about Lady Sheila. "What's Guy's mother like? Will she be difficult, do you think?"

"Lady Sheila is truly a Lady. I always found her to be kind and generous. It's Ellen her maid who'll give us a hard time. She used to be nanny to Guy and me. She made us toe the line." He drank the last of his tea and we hurried back to our various jobs.

I took Mick and Rick away from their grouting long enough to have them help Harry move the gold and ivory furniture into the parlor. Things began to fall into place and as John came up the drive with our guests, I hung a gold-framed painting of someone's scowling ancestor on the east parlor wall and arranged some china figurines on the mantel. One last pat to a burgundy pillow and we were ready.

Lady McLeod looked like an elderly princess as John helped her out of the Land Rover. She might have descended from a golden carriage the way she put her gloved fingers over his arm and let him lead her into the house. She greeted me graciously and we escorted her down the hall to the newly decorated suite.

Before we withdrew I nodded politely. I had to resist the impulse to curtsy. "Perhaps you'd like to come to the parlor for tea in about thirty minutes."

She smiled at me. "Thank you my dear." We left her with Ellen, her maid, fussing over coats, scarves, and luggage. There was no mention of a cook or a footman. I bet Guy made them up to tease me.

I cleaned up, put on a skirt and blouse, and combed my hair. In exactly a half hour Lady McLeod appeared in the great hall and walked to the parlor, ready for her tea. I felt so proud of Jilly as she carried in the heavy tray. It wasn't silver or anything fancy but there were so many wee sandwiches and frosted cakes you couldn't tell it was only enameled tin. I'd unpacked the new, orchard gold china, which set a nice tone.

"Lady McLeod, this is Jilly Burns. She and her husband, Harry, are excellent furniture refinishers and painters. Right now they're working on the third floor." As I introduced Jilly I noted that she looked a bit more plump than when she first came. Well, all of us on the staff were eating well since Jilly took over most of the cooking.

John and I chatted about the weather and asked Lady Sheila about her trip. "The train journey is a long one but I yearned to see this house. I visited here right after Guy purchased it and I'm amazed at what you've done. My rooms are lovely and even Ellen acted impressed. By the way, where is she to stay?"

We'd struggled with this and decided to turn the master suite study into the maid's room. We kept it simple and maid like but it looked attractive and would be quite convenient. I'd decorated it with the plaids and paisleys that we stole from a third-floor room, and it seemed just right for the crotchety old lady.

I felt extremely nervous about how Lady McLeod would fit into our household, but she seemed comfortable sharing tea with John and me. I hesitantly asked her a few questions. "Ma'am, where would you like your other meals served? The dining room is our command central or office for the project. We all eat in the morning room together and we share the cooking. Jilly's our main cook and you're free to discuss menus with her."

"Oh, my dear, I don't want any extra fuss made over me. Ellen can prepare my breakfast and bring a tray to my room. I'd like to join you for the other meals in the morning room. I'll eat what you have and enjoy it. Will that be all right?"

I couldn't believe how easy she was making her stay with us. "Of course it will. Dinner will be at seven o'clock this evening. Perhaps you'd like to rest after your journey."

"I'll go to bed early tonight, rather than go to my room now. What I'd really like is a tour of the entire house to see your progress. May we do that?"

I poured a last cup of tea for each of us. "Oh yes, we surely can. Do you want John or me to take you around?"

"I want you, my dear. I know from Guy's telephone calls that you've provided all the ideas for the decorating so I want you to show me the rooms." Well at least he called his mother. I'd likely slipped off his list of people to contact.

I started out feeling dreadfully nervous as I guided Lady Sheila over the house, but her Ladyship seemed so at ease that I began to relax. She admired the colors and designs. There were no criticisms and her compliments were most pleasant. By the time we'd done the grand tour from basement to fourth floor Jilly called us to dinner.

Lady McLeod settled right into our household. At mealtime she managed to get conversation out of Harry, who never used two words when one would do. He actually became chatty that first evening as he helped himself to his fourth lamb chop.

The only change the two newcomers made in our routines was due to Ellen's contrary nature. She would appear in my workroom, clear her throat, and give me a watery smile. "Miss, I really do think her Ladyship shouldn't have to eat with the servants. I would be most happy to serve her meals on a tray in her own sitting room."

"Lady McLeod chose to eat with the staff, Ellen. I rather think she likes the company of the young people. You know you are welcome to join us for meals too."

That brought forth a severe sniff and she refused with a haughty turn of her head. "I know my place, Miss Glenna, and that's more than I can say for others." Of course Ellen's solitary meals in the kitchen caused more work than if she'd shared our table.

Ellen turned out to be the fly in the jam pot. Almost every day she'd track me down to offer her ridiculous complaints. All of us struggled to put up with her but she tried everyone's patience. Every minute she wasn't fussing over Lady Sheila she crocheted large doilies. Soon all flat surfaces in the master suite disappeared under a deluge of lacy-white masterpieces.

Ellen's behavior and the continued lack of a phone call from Guy kept me on edge and a bit worried, but before long something else came along to divert my mind.

CHAPTER 12

One morning at breakfast Jilly drained her teacup and fixed her brown eyes on me. "Miss Glenna, can Harry and me have next Saturday afternoon off?"

"You certainly may. You haven't taken off all the time you've earned. Do you have something special you want to do?" I wasn't prying, just interested.

Harry lifted his head from his plate of porridge. "It's a bit special, miss. We're going to get married. I saw the rector at the village kirk and he's announced the banns the last three Sundays. We're set for two o'clock Saturday next."

"My word. Will your families come for the ceremony?"

Harry nodded. "Me mum, she's coming from our farm near York, and maybe me brother, Peter, to stand up with me."

"Well, how exciting. And what about your people, Jilly?"

She gave me a shy smile. "Me dad and me brother, Jim, said they'd come along from Hull. We've been saving our money to have them to dinner at the Crown and Anchor afterward. And, Miss Glenna would you come and stand up with me for the part at the church?"

"I'll be pleased to, Jilly. Do you have a dress to wear?"

"Not really. None of me good clothes fit anymore. I need to run into a shop in town and see if I can find something."

Then it hit me. Jilly was pregnant. Hence, the rushed wedding and the outgrown clothes. She hadn't gained weight from eating. A baby had caused her face to become more round and her tummy to swell. This called for us to rally around and make the wedding special.

"First, yes you can have all of next Saturday off. Second, I'm honored to stand up with you. Third, did you know there are some trunks upstairs full of old clothing? Maybe we can find you an old-fashioned dress that would look festive enough for a wedding."

The rest of that week ratcheted up to frantic. We kept on with our regular work but the wedding rose to number one in everyone's mind. One of the attic trunks contained an ivory lawn dress from the thirties, with a handkerchief hemline and princess yoke. Jilly washed it and hung it to bleach in the sunshine. Before we knew it Ellen snatched the dress off the line to mend a few rips and tears. She also unearthed a piece of cobwebby old lace for Jilly's veil and ironed the garments.

I went through my wardrobe searching for something appropriate for a bridesmaid to wear. I unearthed a sheer green skirt with a darker green blouse. It would do after Ellen pressed out the wrinkles.

Harry stood so tall and thin that we despaired of dressing him. Nothing of John's came close to being long enough. Then Harry mentioned casually that he had a pair of gray dress trousers that were only a couple of inches too short. "I wore 'em when I played trumpet in the town band the other year." The attic yielded a gray striped morning coat from the 1920's, a ruffled shirt, and a gray bow tie. The coat sleeves didn't quite cover his wrists, but the fit came close otherwise and he would do. When his brother appeared in a plain dark suit we were set.

Lady McLeod insisted she would provide the wedding dinner so instead of going to the pub, the pub came to us, complete with a lavish buffet and a girl to serve. John contributed a couple of magnums of champagne and several bottles of beer in case some of the guests preferred it.

I made a supreme effort and cleared all my samples, notes, and plans out of the dining room. The big old table would seat twenty and enough orchard-gold dinnerware waited in the cupboard to serve us nicely. Ellen dug a linen tablecloth out of an attic drawer, which she bleached and ironed. I don't know how we'd function without the treasures in the attic. With some flowers, the table looked lovely.

Jilly's dad gave her away in a charming manner. When the vicar asked who gives this woman, he responded with a smile. "Her mother, rest her soul, and I do." It made for a sweet ceremony and I felt a couple of tears slip down my cheeks at the end. Then Harry gave her the kiss of her life and we all laughed and enjoyed it.

Harry's mother seemed a no-nonsense woman, but I noticed her shy smile during the toasts at the wedding feast. Harry's brother kept as silent as Harry but he grinned a lot. I fell for Jilly's dad. He looked like a teddy bear of a man and passed out hugs indiscriminately. Her brother came from the same mold and we had a jolly time.

The Jardine boys turned up at the church stuffed into tweed suits a little on the small side. Their wives wore simple dresses and coats, but sported splendid hats, covered with a few too many artificial fruits and flowers. All four of them adored the champagne and John made a trip to the wine cellar to supplement the refreshments from the Laird's supply.

The wedding party turned into a wild success and when the guests made going home gestures, Jilly threw her arms around me and spoke with tears in her eyes. "What a wonderful day, Miss Glenna. I never figured Harry and me would have such a fine wedding. Thanks for everything. We'll go now but we'll be back tomorrow."

"Don't rush, you two. Just enjoy yourselves." I'd sprung for a night at the local inn for them and John drove them there after hugs all around.

Jilly's dad and brother took a bit too much of the drink so John escorted them up to Jilly and Harry's room to sleep it off. We urged Harry's family to stay too but his mother spoke firmly. "We have our farm truck and we'll just drive on north to York tonight."

We all urged them to stay. "You'll get too sleepy on the road." But they insisted on going, so we waved them on their way. Lady McLeod looked quite done-in, and Ellen whisked her off to bed. The Jardines asked to show their wives some of the rooms they'd painted but at length we got them out the door.

John and I looked at each other. We both said, "Tea," at the same time and ran for the kitchen. We brought a tray up by the fireplace and ate leftover wedding cake.

"I'm so pleased with how the ceremony went." I love to hold a post mortem after a wedding. I usually discuss all the details with a woman friend but John would have to put up with me. "Jilly looked stunning. She really is a beautiful girl with her dark hair and eyes. I wonder who the baby will look like."

"Baby!" John burst out. "Who's having a baby?"

"Why, Jilly and Harry. I assumed you'd noticed. Certainly Lady McLeod and Ellen have figured it out. I think it'll arrive in late November or early December."

"Well, won't that mess us up getting the work done? How can Jilly cook and paint when she's pregnant? And later she'll have the baby to care for. We'll have to replace her."

"Now, don't go off half-cocked, John. Mothers manage to have babies and work too. I agree that we need to lighten her workload soon and she shouldn't breathe the varnish remover or paint fumes any longer. But she doesn't have to sit around on a satin pillow while she waits for the baby. She needs mild exercise and at least the cooking to keep her busy."

"I can't get over it. Am I the last one to know?"

"Probably. You can bet the Jardine ladies spotted all the signs."

When John went off to bed that night he looked terribly befuddled. I laughed at him, and that didn't help his mood.

The next morning I apologized and he accepted it gracefully. "Please no more secrets. I beg you to keep me better informed."

I raised my hand and swore solemnly. "I promise not to leave you out of the loop in the future."

CHAPTER 13

Late fall came upon us and things seemed awfully quiet after the excitement of the wedding. Guy never called John or me. We knew he did phone his mother, because she would report on him occasionally. "My wandering son flew to Tokyo this week," or "Guy called from Houston, Texas, last evening."

We would ask a few questions, but Guy reported little real news to his mother. I told myself that I counted for nothing but a one-night stand and that I must forget my globetrotting boss. We'd turned into a tight little family in Hollystone House and I felt secure there. Even crusty Ellen unbent enough to join us in the morning room for meals. Since she knew about the baby, she acted almost human. John had to drive her to the village to purchase yarn and she spent her spare time knitting wee booties and sweaters.

One night or actually morning, as it was about three o'clock, in late November, Harry woke John, and asked him to drive Jilly to the nursing home where they'd arranged for the baby's birth. John came to my room before they left. "I'm taking Harry and Jilly along to the hospital. I suppose I'll return in a bit."

He ended up staying with Harry and called back occasionally with reports. "I never knew how long this would take, Glennie. Harry looks pale around the gills and so do I."

Lady Sheila, Ellen, and I spent a restless time waiting for news. I couldn't seem to stick to any activity that day. Every time the phone rang we'd drop what we were doing and rush to see if it brought news of Jilly and the baby.

About nine in the evening John and Harry came in the door with their collars askew, both of them talking at once.

"The baby weighs eight pounds and two ounces."

"He looks like Jilly with her brown eyes and he sports a mop of dark curly hair."

"His name is James Ford Burns."

John burst with eagerness to explain. "Do ye get it, Glennie? He's named after us. James for you and Ford from Fordyce. Isn't that clever?"

"I'm bowled over. This is the most flattering thing that's ever happened to me in my entire life."

I had the tea tray ready and we celebrated with sweet cakes in the morning room. Even Ellen toasted the child with her teacup. After the older women and Harry went off to bed, I made John tell me all about the events at the nursing home.

"Harry turned into a nervous wreck and I wasn't much better. At first I intended to come home, but he looked so undone I thought I better stay and give him a bit of support. I never waited that long for anything in my life. The hours crept along minute by slow minute. I just knew nothing would ever happen. Once in a while a nurse came out with a progress report. A few times they let Harry in to see Jilly but then they shooed him right out again."

"It must have been horrible. Did Harry get upset?"

"By early evening we both were on the ragged edge. I guess we drank about a dozen cups of coffee apiece. I had just made up my mind to go hunt up somebody and ask for a report when this doctor chap came out and said Jilly had produced a boy. I waited some more while Harry went in to see Jilly. He came out grinning like a Cheshire cat and said they were sending him home so Jilly could sleep."

The next day Lady Sheila, John, and I crowded into the cab of the truck and took Jilly some flowers from the village shop. They let us see her for five minutes and then said she needed her rest. However, they allowed us to stand in front of the corridor window and look at the little fellow as long as we wanted. Lady Sheila seemed enchanted with little James. "Isn't he a darling? Will we be calling him Jamie, do you suppose?"

"I can't get over him having all that dark curly hair. I thought all babies came into the world bald," John said.

I added my two cents worth. "My three nephews hadn't a hair on their heads when they were born. They have mops of red hair like mine now, but my brother thought they'd look like little old men all their lives."

Lady Sheila put her hand on John's arm. "Don't you think it's time you married and had a child of your own, John?"

He looked surprised and a bit flustered. "Don't rush me, ma'am. I'm not sure I'm up to what Harry went through last night."

When we returned to the house, John gave Harry the truck keys and sent him off for his visit. I began to worry that the Burnses had very little in the way of baby equipment. "John, we've got to do something. That baby doesn't have a crib to sleep in. Harry picked up an infant basket at the junk store in town. Do you recall? He painted it pale yellow and then added tiny flowers on the handle and scattered over the wicker surface. It's really sweet, but babies grow fast and in a few weeks he'll need a proper bed."

John seemed worn-out from his long night and day with Harry. "So what is it you want me to do?"

"We need to find a store and get that child a real bed. It could be a joint gift from us both, or from Hollystone or something. What do you think?"

He gave me a dour look. "I think we better wait till Harry comes back with the truck as it's our only transport."

"We have a few days till it'll be needed, but then we must do something."

He nodded at me. "Right. In a few days we'll do something."

"In the meantime, Mr. Fordyce, is a nap in order? You sound a bit grumpy."

"I'll slip away to my room and catch a few winks. See you at tea time."

A day later Harry brought Jilly and little Jamie home in that awful truck. Why could no one around here afford a decent car?

Ellen stormed around the house, fretting and grumbling. "It's far too soon for a new mother to leave the nursing home. Jilly will lose her milk and have female complaints the rest of her life. Mark my words and see if she doesn't."

Lady Sheila spoke in a soothing voice. "I'm sure the doctors know what they're doing. We must not interfere." She followed this with a stern look at Ellen who ducked her head.

The rest of us were afraid to touch the baby. He seemed so fragile, although at his weight, I guess he was pretty tough.

The others gave no thought to celebrating Thanksgiving since it isn't a British holiday. However I loved that day with all the good food. I told the others we were celebrating Thanksgiving because we were thankful that Jilly and Baby Jamie came through his birth with no difficulties. I cooked a special dinner for the occasion. It lacked a bit of being up to Jilly's standard, but the turkey was tender and the mountain of mashed potatoes disappeared completely. Actually John peeled the potatoes. I cleared all the fabric samples off the dining room table and it felt as if we were a family when we sat down to our feast.

The work on the house went on. The baby made a few changes in our routine but mostly he just fit into the household. We made sure Jilly didn't overdo and let Harry and the Jardines carry on with the painting while she rested. They were doing a faux finish in the dining room. The bottom half of the walls was a deep olive green and the top area was faux painted a faded gold and green with metallic touches. The border that linked the two halves was decorated with richly colored fruit. We found some matching fabric and John, armed with a staple gun, helped me reupholster the eighteen dining room chairs.

That had its dramatic moments. John grabbed the first piece of fabric. He struggled and tugged and swore. With his face as red as fire, he yelled at me. "Blast it, Glennie, this piece is just too bloody small. Let me see your measurements and the tape."

I meekly handed over the measuring tape and held one end for him.

His frown deepened as he studied the piece. "Now look, it should be twenty-one inches square, and you cut it nineteen and a half. Where is your head, woman? Pay attention to what you're doing."

I humbly cut another square of fabric and handed it over. It fit perfectly and the operation progressed smoothly for a while. When John tackled chair number fifteen, he managed to staple his left forefinger to the padded seat board. The staple gun was electric, the staples were extra large, and it nailed him tight. "John, we've got to pry the staple loose. We better take you to a doctor."

"My God, I don't need a doctor. Find a big screwdriver and pry up on the bugger."

Harry heard us and came into the hall. "Mr. John, we should take you to the doctor. I don't like the looks of that blood oozing from your finger. Puncture wounds get infected."

John spoke through clenched teeth. "I'm not going to the doctor. Get Mick Jardine from the dining room. Tell him to bring his biggest screwdriver or a small pry bar. That might be better."

Both Jardines clumped into the hall bringing their entire toolbox. Mick marched up to John. "What's the problem here, Mr. John? Oh, I see the trouble. That's a bad un'. You want I should give er' a pry with this here little lever?"

"Yes. Just do it. I feel like a damn fool hooked to this board and I'm bleeding all over the new cover."

The tool looked clean and besides how could we disinfect John's finger with him attached to the board?

Mick stepped up manfully, ready to operate. He nodded at his brother. "Rick, just you put your hands on the man's shoulders to steady him like."

By this time Lady Sheila and Jilly drifted in to join the crowd and we all watched, holding our collective breaths. Mick slipped the small tool under the tip of John's finger and pried up abruptly. The staple let go of the board but stayed in the finger. John groaned.

I moved in closer to get a good look. "Mick, do you have a pair of needle-nose pliers in your box? We could use them to grip the staple and lift it free of the finger."

"Sure, Miss Glennie. Her's got the right idea, don't she, Rick? Here's them little pliers, a tad greasy but I'll give em' a bit of a wipe with me rag. Now then sir, one more tug and she'll be over."

By this time John's face had turned a pasty color and I hoped he could hang on till the deed was done. Mick expertly gripped the staple. With one quick motion he yanked it out and laid it on the table. John took one look at the blood welling out of the two puncture wounds and turned a pale green. Harry quickly forced John's head between his knees and averted a faint.

I gave Jilly a nod. "This looks like a good time for a tea break. Get some up here as fast as you can. Harry, why don't you help her?" I stepped into the library where I knew John had stashed a bottle of whiskey. I splashed a couple of inches into a tumbler and came out to the hall in time to watch John lift his head and stare at us with a dazed look.

"Here, John, drink this." He grabbed onto the glass with both hands and swallowed the whiskey neat. He gasped and tears came to his eyes, but he manfully sat up straight. "All right, show's over. Everyone back to work."

"Maybe we could have our tea now," I said. "But first you better come along and let me wash your hand and cover the wound with a bandage."

"Quit fussing, Glenna. I'm fine."

Mick took a serious look at John's hand. "Us thinks her is right, mister. You go along and get fixed up and then us will have our tea."

I led John to the cloakroom. "Wash your hands with soap first." I patted his hand dry with paper towels and applied a large Band-Aid.

"Thanks, Glennie. I feel like a fool to cause so much fuss. Come on, I really need that cup of tea." Harry quietly finished upholstering the chairs after John went to bed that night. A local woman made the matching draperies and with the laying of dark-gold carpet like that in the parlor, the dining room looked ready for a banquet.

The big surprise came when Ellen took over the baby's care. Seems the family'd hired her as Mr. Guy and Mr. John's nurse all those years ago. "Och, I do love the wee bairns." When Ellen busied herself with hand laundry or mending for her mistress, we would often find Jamie resting in Lady Sheila's lap while she made the rocking chair hum.

We welcomed the day when Jilly went back to the kitchen to cook at least one meal a day. At first we made sure that one of us carried the food up from the kitchen and did the cleanup. I scarcely believed how my life as an independent bachelor girl changed to being part of a family.

CHAPTER 14

One busy day a few weeks after the baby arrived I answered the bell at the double front doors. We were expecting a delivery from Harrods so it stunned me to find my parents standing there with luggage in hand. I wrote to them after I arrived at Hollystone House and gave them an address and phone number. The only correspondence they'd sent were letters that alternated between ordering me to come home and begging me to give up my wayward life. I stopped opening them after the first three arrived. I figured that by this time they'd written me out of the will and disinherited me forever.

Mother threw herself on me and sobbed brokenly. "Glennie, we simply had to come and see if you were in any trouble. We imagined you in some unsavory place with all sorts of inappropriate people." Dad kept ineffectually patting her shoulder. Rage coursed through my veins! When would these people let me grow up?

The wailing and confusion drew everyone to the great hall. Ellen strode in with the baby over her shoulder and sternly shushed us.

Lady Sheila, enjoying a quiet time reading in the parlor poked her head around the doorway. John stopped shelving books in the library and came into the hall. I drew in a deep breath and wondered what to do next. He took in the situation and immediately stepped in to help me.

"Mr. and Mrs. James, welcome to Hollystone House. May I present Lady Sheila McLeod? And this is Ellen Greer, our nanny. The baby's parents are part of our redecorating staff and I'm Miss Glenna's assistant, John Fordyce."

The folks gaped at the assembled group and began to look embarrassed. Mom wrung her hands and looked from face to face. "Excuse us for barging in but we were so worried about Glennie. We didn't want her to take this job and we felt compelled to come and see whether she was safe. Actually we intend that she return home with us."

Lady Sheila defended me most eloquently. "I wish I had a daughter like Glenna. She works so hard and is such a clever lassie. Please will you join us in the parlor for tea? Glennie, I'll show them the way, if you'll alert Jilly." Bless her heart. If anything would impress my parents, it was this woman who looked every inch a lady. And I had to smile. My mother detests tea but she felt so in awe of her Ladyship that she gulped down two cups.

I settled Mom and Dad in a far corner of the third floor. Putting them at the opposite end of the house from my room gave me a little freedom from their incessant nagging. Whenever they tracked me down, the same old struggle went on and on. Mom would beam a fake smile at me and lay a hand on my arm. "Glennie, we're going to get you a ticket to fly home with us. It's simply the right thing for you to do."

I'd shake her arm off mine and turn away toward the library, hoping I'd find John in there. Before I could move two steps, Dad would circle around and cut me off. "Glennie, we only have your best interests at heart." I wanted to run screaming down to the first floor just to get away from the nagging.

The week following my parents arrival seemed to last a month. Baby Jamie sensed the tension and he cried long and loud. Ellen complained because the child did his howling at night when Jilly took care of him and she couldn't interfere. She made one of her dire predictions in a gloomy voice. "Mark my words; all this upset will mark that young one."

Jilly became exhausted from lack of sleep and stumbled around the house looking pale and pinched. Harry seemed edgy with worry about his wife. Even the Jardines, Mick and Rick, helping Harry finish up the paint work, stayed quietly on the third floor and drank their tea up there. Normally they sat with us and dined from their dinner pails while we ate lunch.

I turned into a wreck. Every time I spent a minute alone with my folks, they worked on me. "How can you be happy so far from your family?" Mom would ask.

Then Dad would rumble at me in his deep voice. "Your mother has worked herself into a real state and stayed that way ever since you left, Glennie. She wants you at home where she doesn't need to worry about you. It isn't fair for you to cause us this much concern. We expect you to come home with us. We'll fix up your old room and you can stay with us."

As if I'd ever move back into my parents home. I did my best to keep my mouth shut. I mostly listened and let it flow over me but at times I had to let off steam. John became my safety valve. He let me blow my stack and listened to what I had to say. "Glennie, somehow that name suits you better than Glenna; anyway you've made the break from your parents. You're established here and making a great success of your work. Bite your tongue and stand your ground. Your parents will soon be gone and they can't physically force you to leave with them. We all understand the pressure you're under and will divert it when we can."

Lady Sheila gave me wonderful support. She knew what the folks put me through and kept taking Mom and Dad into the parlor for chats and cups of tea to get them off my back. She hired a car and driver on two different days and took them to see the sights. Oh, how I appreciated her support.

One day I overheard Lady Sheila talking to the folks. "But you can't take our Glennie. She's the glue that holds this household together. And of course we can't overlook her contract with my son. I'm sure he expects her to complete the work he engaged her to do."

By the end of the week the strain left me barely able to function. I could hardly choke down food and I slept in fits and starts. I'd dream mother was leaning over my bed and then I'd wake to toss and turn. I lived on cups of tea, lost five pounds, and my face began to look as if I were a war refugee. Early one morning I sat in the morning room with a mug of tea clutched in my hands.

John came in and grabbed a chair. "Glennie, this can't go on. I'm truly worried about you. It's time we sent your parents home and allowed you to get back to a normal life. How can I help you?"

"Oh, John, you're a dear. I have an idea. Dad, at least, has a very strong work ethic. If you'll tell him they're jeopardizing my job, he may accept that and take Mother home. You could say something like, 'Lord Guy will arrive soon so we have to have the third floor finished by the holidays.' Then frown a bit and act as if Guy is a hard taskmaster."

"Will do. I can lay it on thick and indicate that we walk on eggs when Guy arrives. Lady Sheila will very likely help us. Let's set it up for lunch today."

"Great. If you talk to her Ladyship I'll see what I can dig up for us to eat. I'll be so glad when Jilly can take over the cooking full time. She has a real knack in the kitchen that I don't seem to possess."

I opened three tins of potato soup, browned an onion, and diced some leftover ham to toss in the soup pot. From the pantry I unearthed a box of pilot crackers and opened a jar of cheese spread to go with them. Canned peaches and cookies would fill in the cracks. As I dished up the soup the front bell rang and whoever arrived made a great commotion. John had answered the door and I could hear the noise move my way.

Guy McLeod walked into the morning room and my parents followed right behind him. He came straight toward me, crushed me in a dramatic hug, and gave me a great smacking kiss. I expected the folks to act very upset by this, but no. They beamed at me as if I'd finally done the right thing.

It sickened me the way Mother gushed at him. "Oh, Lord McLeod, I'm delighted to meet you." I thought she was actually on the verge of a curtsy.

John told me when I came that Guy didn't want to be addressed as lord. Guy handled it nicely though. "Now, none of that, Mrs. James. We're all friends and family here. Glenna is one of the main stays of our group and my mother thinks the world of her."

He left the room to escort his mother to lunch and my mother climbed all over me.

"Oh, Glennie, he's so handsome. Do you have an understanding?"

"No, Mom. This is the second time I've seen Guy since I got here. He doesn't call, he doesn't write, and he's offered no opportunity for us to get better acquainted. For heavens sake, don't say a word to him. He's my employer and that's all."

All through lunch Mom beamed at Guy. I knew she envisioned me clad in the antique family bridal gown, traipsing down the aisle in the village kirk or perhaps Westminster Abbey. Her dearest wish was to see me safely married to a man who would take care of me.

It didn't matter that a wealthy husband hovered at the bottom of my list. I had no desire for a father figure to take care of me. I wanted a man who would stay home with me, not a gadabout who traveled the world year in and year out.

I hadn't a clue what game Guy was playing, but he set out to charm my parents. Then he would smile fondly at me. It felt like I was wading through a pond of maple syrup. When I cleared the lunch table and took a loaded tray down to the kitchen, Guy followed right along, and so did my mother. He and she actually tussled over the dishtowel, arguing who would dry the dishes. I made up my mind to order a dishwasher first thing Monday morning.

Guy's appearance meant that John and I lost the opportunity to put our plan to work.

At his request I took Guy on a tour of the house. The rooms showed dramatic changes since his previous visit. He acted especially pleased with the dining room. My folks followed us as if they toured our future love nest. Mother cooed over the nursery suite. "Oh, Glenna, wouldn't you love to raise your children in such handsome rooms? You could decorate them with fluffy lambs on a blue background."

My mother has good decorating sense but she surely lacks any other kind of sense. We lost them as we climbed to the fourth floor, when they stopped to catch their breath. As soon as they faded from sight and hearing, I tried to explain the situation to Guy.

"I must apologize for my parents, Guy. They've settled on you as a wonderful son-in-law prospect. Mother's tried to marry me off ever since I graduated from high school. During college my visits home turned into a constant verbal war. 'Did you have a date last Saturday night, dear' or 'Why don't you bring some nice boy along the next time you come home for a weekend?'"

Guy patted my shoulder. "It must have frustrated you terribly, Glenna. If you weren't so upset I'd find the situation humorous."

Despite his attempt to reassure me, I couldn't quit talking about my overbearing family. "If I brought a fella to visit, Dad dragged him off to his workshop to inquire about his intentions. I soon learned not to bring anyone home and answered all questions with negatives. I pretended that I enjoyed no social life and then they scolded me about how I looked. 'You must leave off the jeans and wear your pretty dresses. Couldn't you curl your hair and look more feminine?'"

"Don't fret, Glenna. I understand the fix you're in. John's mother treats him the same way. Thank heavens my mother has more sense than to do that. She desperately wants an heir but she only talks to old Ellen about it. Ellen, of course, gets right onto me about wedding bells and the patter of tiny feet. Let's forget them all. I'm more interested to see if your kisses are as exciting as I remember."

We stepped back into an alcove and he pulled me into his arms. I'd forgotten how dynamic this fellow could be.

"Oh, there you are." Mother managed to arrive on the fourth floor. She saw us in a passionate embrace and it was the answer to her expectations. She must have thought she was tactful as she babbled to Guy. "Lord McLeod, this is the most fantastic house. I'm sure when it's finished you'll settle down here with a wife and children. Won't that be nice?"

I walked down the steps to get away from her. If I stayed near my mother another minute, I'd do something regrettable like scream in her face or actually slap her.

At dinner that evening mother continued her campaign to marry her Glennie to this wealthy, they assumed, Scottish laird. I roasted a leg of lamb, baked some potatoes, and tossed together some limp greens for a salad. Then the barrage began. "What a wonderful dinner." She followed this remark by a smirk in Guy's direction and kept right on talking. "Glennie has always been a good cook. She took to it naturally. I hardly taught her a thing." What you taught me, I thought to myself, was to run for the hills whenever you came near me.

Dear Lady Sheila tried to smooth things over. "Glennie is a good cook. It's been such a treat to have her here and to enjoy the meals she's prepared for us."

I waded in with both feet. "Actually Jilly does most of the cooking. It's only during this bad patch with the baby so fussy that I took over. I believe when things quiet down and there aren't so many people around, the colic will go away and she'll be back in the kitchen. Isn't that right, Jilly?"

"Oh yes, miss. I do enjoy fixing the food. The doctor says Jamie should be over this rough patch soon and we can return to the old schedule."

After I served a rather thin, dry cake for desert, Guy murmured to me in an undertone. "I'd like to have a word with you and John in the library after dinner. We need to talk about some things." I nodded my head and slipped out of my chair to clear the table. Harry and Jilly headed down to the kitchen to put the leftovers away and do the dishes.

Mother grabbed my arm and whispered so everyone could hear. "I'm sure he wants to propose to you. Go brush your hair down and put on some lipstick."

I yanked my arm away, grabbed a tablet and pen from the dining room, and stalked to the library. John joined us there so I knew we were meeting for business.

CHAPTER 15

When Guy and John joined me in the library, I trembled with anger. My mother had overstepped her boundaries and I wouldn't put up with her behavior any longer.

"Guy, I apologize again for Mother. Her sense of what is fitting and what isn't is entirely missing. She's come up a few bricks shy of a load and as soon as our meeting ends, I'll give my parents their walking papers. They have to leave tomorrow morning before we all lose our minds. They've abused the hospitality of this house and I'll tell them so."

Guy and John chatted about inconsequential things while I pulled myself together. When Guy began to speak John and I found his words riveting. "Glenna, John, I have incurred some unexpected expenses and we're looking at some changes here. It's a matter of extending a drilling contract. Now, don't worry that you won't get paid or that the redecorating must stop. It's more of a matter of using Hollystone as an income source. I'm thinking seriously of turning the House into a high-class bed-and-breakfast. I can't afford to heat the place and pay the taxes and insurance while it sits here waiting for me to settle down. As a B and B it could pay for itself and when I'm ready to become a homebody we can convert it back to a stately home."

The news stunned me, but John nodded his head and seemed to understand what our boss said. Guy picked up a pen and tapped it on the desktop. "You two have turned out to be a good team and I'd like for you to organize and manage this new venture. I'll continue your salaries. In fact you don't need to make a profit. Just cover the expenses, including wages, and I'll be satisfied. I'd like Mother and Ellen to stay on here, and if Jilly would remain as cook and Harry take on maintenance, all you'll need to do is hire maids to clean the rooms and launder the bedding. What do you say? Will you give it a go?"

John and I looked at each other for a long minute. Then I nodded and he did the same. I didn't know his reasons but I simply wanted to stay in a situation where I felt happy with people I knew and liked. We'd soon be rid of my folks and I couldn't imagine going home and living near them ever again. Guy seemed satisfied with that. "We'll make some plans in the morning. Glenna, are you ready to go up?"

"Up where?"

"To your room. I hope you'll share your room with me tonight. I had Harry put my bags in there when I arrived."

John looked surprised and angry, and the very idea made me furious. "Guy, aren't you taking some things for granted? I prefer not to share my room with anyone while my parents are still in the house. In fact, I don't want to do that under any circumstances. I'll bid you both good night and see you at breakfast tomorrow. Guy, I'll set your luggage out in the hall."

I flounced up the staircase. The nerve of that jerk. I'd felt all along that I shouldn't have slept with him that night in London and now I knew I'd made a mistake. By this time I felt furious with everyone, Guy for his callous treatment of me, my folks for their interfering ways, and John for just being there. I went directly to my parents' room. I figured I'd better show them the door while I'd built up a head of steam.

I knocked and heard a sleepy voice. "Come in." When I entered the room, Mom bounced up in bed beaming. "Tell us what happened, dear. Oh, I'm so excited. Don't keep us waiting."

"Mom, Dad, you have embarrassed me beyond any hope for a peaceful reconciliation at this time. I can't handle any more stress from your blatant hints about marriage and what a good little homemaker I am. Guy McLeod is my employer only. He's not indicated in any way that he's looking for a wife. Now let me make this very clear. You are not welcome here. Whatever it takes, I want you out of here and on your way to Heathrow tomorrow. If you can't arrange a flight home for a couple of days, you can stay at a hotel while you wait. I'll pay for whatever it takes to get you on your way back to America. I've had enough of your sly innuendos to Lady Sheila and her son. This is goodbye. I'll be busy tomorrow and probably won't see you. You can call a taxi to take you to the train station in the morning."

Mother cried into a Kleenex and Dad turned an unhealthy shade of purple. Mom dropped her tissue and her voice shook when she spoke. "You can't just turn us out. We only have your best interests at heart. We planned to stay here for Christmas and then take you home with us. What will your brother think when we arrive home without you?"

"I don't know, nor do I care. When you come to your senses and quit trying to manage my life, perhaps we can see each other again. Until that time I prefer not to hear from you in any way. Goodbye."

My father put his hands over his face as if to hide from the scene, then dropped them. "But, Glenna, we're only trying to help you."

"No you're not. You're trying to run my life. I don't want your help. Is that clear? You've pushed me too far. I'll say it once more. Tomorrow you leave this house. You are not welcome here."

I flung out of the room and met John in the hallway. The sight of his dear face made me come unglued. I burst into tears and threw myself onto his chest. He opened a door and pulled me into a finished bedroom. He dropped into a chair and settled me on his lap. I slowly stopped sobbing but hung onto him. He felt so solid, so reassuring. When I could speak, I apologized again.

"Glennie, I do understand. My mother has an entire stable of girls that she keeps trotting out for me to marry. I don't go home to Scotland very often because I can't stand the pressure and Mum won't stop."

"You're such a dear man, John. Do you think we can manage a bed and breakfast?"

"I'm sure we can. Why don't I draw up a budget and you can plan what services we'll offer and who will take on which responsibilities. Get some sleep now and let's meet for early tea in the morning."

He stood up, steadied me on my feet, and kissed my cheek. What a comforting man. Why couldn't Guy treat me the way John did.

CHAPTER 16

Since I'd let my anger spill over my parents and shed those tears, I slept well. Waking just before seven, I pulled on jeans and a sweater, combed my hair, and put on a touch of lipstick. When I got to the morning room, John had the tea made and a plate of warm rolls waited on the table. He was writing on a lined yellow pad and looked ready to become a bed-and-breakfast manager.

"Mornin', Glennie. I expect Guy to be down soon. Let's make our lists and be organized for him. Why don't we write down the duties of hotel managers and then divide them up."

I took out my own pad and pen. "That sounds productive to me. I'd like to make the room reservations. We should both work on advertising. There are businesses that keep lists of what's available and refer people to specific lodgings. And what about publications? Before I made the trip over here a few years ago, I called British Travel and they sent me all sorts of hotel brochures and bed-and-breakfast booklets." I thought a minute and then an idea hit me. "Marketing money! We'll have to have some funds to publicize this venture. Will Guy come up with what we need?"

"We can't afford not to advertise. No way will this venture get on the road without greasing its wheels with a marketing scheme. I'll manage the money and keep the books. You and Jilly can work together on the menus and order the food. Shall we serve only breakfast or should dinner be included?"

"I'm a little leery of serving dinner right away. That's a big undertaking and we'd need more staff to serve and wash up. What if we start small and if things go well and we think we can handle it, dinner could be added at a later time. In the meantime we better provide our guests with the names of local restaurants."

At this point Guy came into the room. I wished I could avoid him. Our run-in from last night embarrassed me. I decided the best thing would be to pretend our personal relationship didn't exist. John poured him tea and let him look over our lists. "Have you two discussed room charges?"

John replied, "No, do you have figures in mind?"

"I don't have any idea what's reasonable but this place should be on the high end. I stay in hotels all the time, but most of them are in remote, uncivilized places and couldn't compare to Hollystone House. How can we find out what other places charge?"

I didn't give either of the men a chance to answer. "We'll shop the competition. We get a directory of comparable lodgings and call to inquire about reservations. They give us prices and we reply with a pat answer. We say 'I'll have to check with my husband or wife about the exact date.' Voila! We have the info we need."

"Excellent. I wonder if you two should go and stay in a couple of these places to get ideas. I'll fax you a list of things that most hotels are missing. You better order a raft of luggage racks. We could be very up to date if we offered modem interfaces in the rooms, so the customers could get e-mail and be on the Internet. Or would it be more sensible to have a modem room for the guests to use?"

John had another agenda. "We'll probably have to go to London to get supplies. We'll need more bedding and towels and I'm sure lots of other things. I expect we'll want a large tea set, because if we don't offer dinner, we should serve high tea. Anyway, when we go to shop we can each stay in a different place and take notes."

"Sounds as if you are off and running." Guy beamed at us. "When do you think you can be ready to open?"

John and I looked at each other and shook our heads. I finally gave him an answer. "Give us a little time to get the plans made and see if they'll work. I don't have all the decorating finished. The second floor is practically ready, but guests will need more amenities than we've included. If we begin with only the second floor, we can continue to work on the third after guests start coming to stay. When we're a wild success, we'll see what can be done with those bitty rooms on fourth—you know, the servants' quarters. Will we have to move up there now that this is a money-making place?"

"I suggest you make Harry, Jilly, and Jamie an apartment on fourth. The baby needs his own room. You should each have a decent chamber of your own, wherever you want it. Mother will stay in the master suite. Oh, damn, you'll have to try and get phones for the rooms and what about the telly? Will you put sets in the rooms?"

John and I spoke at once. "No, let's not."

I poured another round of tea. "That would be a big expense. Let's set up a corner of the great hall with comfortable chairs and install a big screen TV. Better have a bar in there too. Plus we'll need some kind of a counter or desk to check in the guests. What if we kept the morning room and the library just for the staff? The butler's pantry will be about right for a phone and modem corner. I expect we'll get more vacationing couples than traveling businessmen so I doubt we need hookups or phones in every room."

"That sounds good. I have every faith that you two will work out the details. I'll transfer some operating cash to you, John, and of course you'll manage it well. Now, Glenna, I'd like to talk to you. Would you get a coat and we'll walk on the grounds?"

I muttered, "Okay," grabbed a jacket, and headed to the front door. Just then Mom and Dad came down the stairs with their luggage. Mom headed straight for me, but I went into the library and shut the door. I meant to hang tough. No reconciliation, no nothing. I guess John called a cab and saw them off.

When I heard them go, I came out and joined Guy for our walk. As we set out through the door by the fireplace I knew I didn't want to talk about personal things. "We'll have to get a sign made so our visitors can find us. That could be costly. Except maybe Harry could make one. He's very talented."

"Glenna, I don't want to talk about the house now. I want to talk about you and me. It stunned me last night when you turned me out of your room in front of John."

"Well, it shocked and embarrassed me when you assumed, in front of John, that I'd welcome you in my room. I've had second thoughts about the night we shared in London. I have no complaints about the time we were together, but I've seriously regretted my rush to jump into bed with you. I broke my own rule that night.

"And what rule is that?"

"I don't hop in and out of bed with every fellow that comes along. You've made no attempt to keep in touch. You strike me as a good-time Charlie. Out for what you can get with no thought for the future."

"I had no idea you weren't in favor of the night we spent together. You seemed pretty enthusiastic to me."

"You should be flattered that I lost my head, but I'm not doing that again. For now, let's be boss and employee. If you want to spend time with me, write, call, or send me e-mails. When you're here we could have dinner out if I'm free — from work, I mean. I want to apologize one more time for my parents. They embarrassed me painfully with their hints and innuendos. I'm sure they shocked Lady Sheila. Anyway, they're gone now and after I know they've flown out of the country, I'll revert to my normal calm self."

"There's no need to apologize. We've told you John's mother acts the same way. Look I'm sorry if I rushed you. We'll play it your way. I'll keep in touch after I leave. And I better get out of here by tonight as things are heating up in Dubai."

"Great. I'll look forward to hearing from you. You know you and John are so different. It's amazing that you're related."

"Yes, his mother is my father's sister. John and I've always been close. Our parents sent us away to boarding school together and then on to Oxford, when we got older. I studied business and John did accounting. He's kept my books since we left university and I assume he'll add the B and B in with the rest."

"Interesting." A chill wind blew through the trees and I stuffed my hands in my coat pockets. "Well, you need to be on your way so don't forget us out here in the country. You could e-mail your ideas and we'll let you know our plans as we work out the details."

"Glenna, I want you to know how pleased I am with your work on the house. You've come through just as I knew you would. Mother thinks you're a wonder. Now, does our new relationship include goodbye kisses?"

I made no answer, but turned my face toward him and he planted one of those spine-tingling kisses on my lips. It lasted long enough that I became breathless and had one tiny moment of regret about turning him down the night before.

CHAPTER 17

With the folks and Guy gone the house began to run smoothly again. Baby Jamie seemed to know that the source of tension had disappeared and he settled down to be a fat, happy cherub. I'm convinced that old Ellen spoiled him rotten but he seemed to thrive on the attention.

John and I worked daily on the plans for the bed-and-breakfast. We wrote pages of notes, created large lists of items to purchase, and made many phone calls. One morning over our perpetual cups of tea we discussed a trip to London to shop.

"Glennie, do you realize that it's only two weeks until Christmas?"

"It can't be. Whatever happened to November?"

John grabbed the last scone off the tray. "It melted away on us but let's combine this jaunt and do our Christmas shopping. We can each stay in a different inn and get some research done."

"You rat! Give me a bite." I grabbed half the scone and crammed it in my mouth. "Sounds good to me. What day shall we go? And can we stay two nights? I really think we'll need that much time."

"Today is Saturday. Let's leave tomorrow afternoon and get to the city in time to see a show."

"We're cramming a lot of activity into this trip. I'm game but don't complain to me later about overload. I have here a booklet that lists all the inns and bed-and-breakfasts in London. We can stick a pin through the lists and stay where the pages are pricked or be scientific and choose locations fairly close together and in our proposed price range."

"The latter makes more sense to me. You go ahead and choose four for us to try. I'll look into theater tickets. Get packed and we'll take the three forty-five train tomorrow afternoon."

When Harry drove us to the train station, we were ready to assault the city. It felt pleasant to relax as the train rumbled through the many west side London suburbs. For the first time since we started our project, we could sit and talk. I had to tell him what I thought. "Every once in a while I wonder, what are we doing? Neither one of us has any background for running a country inn. Can we really pull this off?"

"Of course we can. As I watched you work on the house, I became convinced you could do anything. Nothing slows you down — well, except your parents. We'll do fine. What one of us forgets, the other will remember."

I smiled at him. "I do hope you're right. Did you get show tickets?"

John dug in his pocket and pulled out an e-mail theater confirmation. "It's called *The Lion King*. Supposed to be the hottest thing in town. I hope you like it." He looked at me with an anxious expression on his face. It was obvious he wanted to please me. "Would you rather see *Chicago*?"

"Since I lived on the fringes of that city I saw the show when it first came out. I loved it but I'd rather go to something I haven't seen. And I've been longing to see *Lion King*."

Our conversation lagged and I was deep in thought when John spoke. "Are you upset with Guy and his everlasting travel? I can tell it bothers you when he doesn't call."

"Guy's an interesting person but frankly I wonder if there's much depth to him. I shouldn't say this but I'm beginning to think he's rather superficial. Either that or he has a very one-track mind. What do you think?"

"Both are good possibilities. He's rather buttoned down, doesn't show a lot of emotion. I've spent a lot of time with him but I'll never understand him."

We taxied to our lodgings from Euston Station. I'd picked two hotels in the same block. We arranged to meet and walk to a nearby hotel that served high tea. But first we checked out our rooms.

It appeared that my hotel was converted from a large old house. My heart sank as I entered the lobby. The tile floor felt gritty under foot and the desk clerk looked like a refugee from a low-budget flophouse. As I struggled up the narrow stairs to the fourth floor, it struck me that we should install an elevator for elderly and infirm guests. Would the budget stretch to that expense?

The room ranked right up there at mediocre. It looked clean but oh, so small. There wasn't a place to put my suitcase and hardly room to set it on the floor. Fortunately Hollystone House had spacious rooms.

John called me from the lobby and I directed him to my room. "This place is pretty bad, Glennie. You should trade with me. Mine is clean and roomy."

"I'm jealous but I can stand one night here. Maybe the breakfast will make up for it."

"Come on, we need to hurry. On Sunday it's an early performance. We'll enjoy tea now and dinner afterward."

The show delighted us and we loved the wonderful songs. We walked out humming bits of music and John led me to a small basement pub that did wonderful steaks.

"How'd you find this place? I love it."

"When my student days were over, I apprenticed with a large accounting firm in London. I lived near here for five years and learned a lot about the city."

I tried to pay my share of the tab but John puffed up indignantly. "I'm not destitute, Glenna." He sounded just like Guy. I guess these English men never heard of going Dutch. "Besides the fact that I earn a decent salary, my father left me enough money to take a young lady out for the evening. Please, no more of this nonsense. Besides, I plan to put it on our expense account. After all, we're here on business."

We walked back to our lodgings and I took a quick tour of his accommodations. "This place is much better than mine, but it's still on the small side. I'm glad our rooms at Hollystone are more spacious. I do like how they've arranged the bath and shower here. Oh, do you think we can afford an elevator?"

"I'll do some figuring when we get home and let you know."

"I better skip down the street and get to my room. See you tomorrow, John. Thanks for a fun evening." I gave him a quick kiss on the cheek and made for the door.

"Oh, no you don't, young lady. I'm not about to let you out on the streets of London by yourself, not at night anyway."

"It's only a block. I'm not afraid."

"Well, I am. This is one of the largest cities in the world and it's full of all types of lowlife. I'll see you to your room!"

John escorted me back to my hotel with great firmness. As we stood outside the main door saying good night, he slipped an arm around my shoulder and gave me a sideways hug. It felt very brotherly but I liked the warmth I felt coming from him. I knew I could depend on John. In thinking it over later, I decided we'd had a delightful evening. In comparing it to the night I spent in London with Guy, I decided I'd enjoyed the evening with John more.

I could barely choke down my breakfast, as the eggs were cold and rock hard. The coffee tasted okay but I should have ordered tea. When we met that morning, we divided up our list so John shopped for luggage racks and other bits of furniture we needed. I had the sheet and towel agenda. I found the B and B association and the clerks immediately deluged me with catalogs and sales literature. I ferreted out an address for a place to buy tissues and those wee bottles of shampoo, lotion, and mouthwash, plus miniature bars of soap.

Our kitchen would need a large and simple-to-use coffeemaker. I better look for a Bunn that brewed by the drip method. The type with multiple pots would be the best choice. Wondering where to purchase one, I went from store to store with my yard-long list.

In a shop that featured odd lots of china I found enough of a sunflower pattern to take care of serving breakfasts. Farther down the street a tea set in a store window caught my eye. It had a large teapot and all the accessories. The set displayed dainty flowers in pastel shades mixed with olive green leaves on a cream background. Each cup showed a different flower in one of a variety of colors. Just the thing for afternoon tea.

This store sold stainless steel flatware too. I chose a simple design that would come out of the dishwasher in good shape. Speaking of which, I hoped John had crossed dishwasher off his shopping list. Surely he'd remember that we'd already installed one.

The fun part of the day's shopping turned out to be choosing Christmas presents. For baby Jamie, I found small denim overalls and a red T-shirt. A teddy bear, with a hidden music box that played lullabies, insisted on going home with me. Ellen rated a capacious, black leather purse. Her old faithful handbag showed its age with cracks and worn places. I hoped Lady Sheila would enjoy a cuddly cream-colored shawl.

Wisely I'd purchased gifts for my brother and his family in early October and mailed the packages in a timely manner. I also sent Michael a check to buy gift certificates for our parents. It felt awkward to plan their gifts when I didn't want to even think about them.

I did call Michael after the folks left and explained what happened. He felt I'd been rather rash. "Sis, I understand where you're coming from. Sometimes Sarah just can't stand all the free advice Mom hands out."

CHAPTER 18

When I couldn't walk another step and was simply dying for a cup of tea, I grabbed my suitcase from last night's lodging and moved two blocks down the street. This time I made a better choice. The lobby looked spacious, clean, and nicely decorated. My room had all the amenities I could want, including an electric teapot with real cream in a small fridge.

John dragged into my room with his tongue hanging out. He looked so tired that I fixed him a cup of tea immediately. He brought a bag of buttered scones for us to share, and they tasted heavenly. After he'd swallowed half his tea in one gulp, I quizzed him. "So, how did your day go? Is everything crossed off your list?"

"Don't try to be funny, Glennie. I'm too far gone for levity. I've spent an enormous amount of money and all I have to show for it is this bag of scones. Actually the delivery vans will be making daily trips to Hollystone for the next month. Now, give me a report on your day."

"I spent a ton of green stuff too. There is something so exciting about flinging around other people's money. When I said I would take six-dozen towels and a carload of bedding the clerks rushed to wait on me. Six-dozen linen napkins will be on hand to serve breakfast and tea. Oh, and I ordered matching tablecloths to use on those little tables we're setting up in the hall."

"Well done, Glennie. What else did you purchase?"

"From a nifty little business called Luxuries for You I bought oodles of facial tissues, a gross of shampoos, and another of skin lotions. I'm afraid I got carried away. I just love those tiny one-shot bottles and jars. The ones I ordered have gold crowns for lids and are classy beyond anything you'd dream about."

The tea and scones helped John because he laughed at some of my stories about the day. Truthfully I think he'd been on the edge of total collapse. Men have no understanding of how to shop. "John, why don't you go to your room for a nap? We'll both rest and then go out and find some dinner."

"Good idea. Could I just lie on your bed for a minute? I need to find enough strength to so I can walk across the street."

That minute was a mistake because he fell into a deep sleep right there and didn't move for two hours. I felt too softhearted to wake him so I left him alone to nap. I dozed in my chair and woke at 7:30. John lay on his back snoring softly. I hauled out the phone book and ordered a large super supreme pizza to be delivered to the room. I had no idea whether John liked pizza, but I'd find out shortly.

When the delivery boy knocked on the door, John roused, sat up straight, and blinked his eyes. "Just resting my eyes. I should go to my room now.

I made us another pot of tea and handed him a slice of the most delectable smelling pizza. He took a large bite and a huge grin appeared on his face. Who would think of going to London for great pizza?

"Glennie, I haven't eaten any since I lived here but I adore it. Can I have more?"

"You can have all you want. I've been living without pizza for far too long. Thank God, you Brits aren't too stuffy to try something different."

We ate all but two pieces and John looked as if another deep sleep was coming on him.

"Perhaps you better find your hotel. It's okay for you to snooze in my room, but sleeping here is another thing altogether. Your lodging is only across the street. Do you want me to escort you over there? I'm afraid you'll walk out in front of a bus."

"I can make it. Thanks for a restful evening and a wonderful supper. Sorry to play out on you but I'm not used to this. I'd rather dig ditches than plow through all those stores." He stood, leaned down, and gave me a light kiss on my cheek. "Why don't I meet you in the lobby here about nine tomorrow morning? I think we can finish up what's left on our lists together. I'd like to get the three o'clock train back to the village in the afternoon. Will that work for you?"

"It will. See you in the morning, John."

"Good night, Glennie."

I'd picked myself a much better bed-and-breakfast our second night in London and I awoke rested and ready to do the final shopping. I'd had my fill of the eggs, sausage, and baked tomato, which seemed to be typical of the "free" breakfasts in all British hotels. I couldn't wait to get back to Hollystone and have scones with blackberry jam and clotted cream. Which reminded me that Jilly and I had menus to plan for our gourmet breakfasts and luscious high teas. There would be none of the ordinary B-and-B items in Hollystone House's breakfasts.

John waited for me while I checked out. "Why don't we take our luggage to the train station and put it in a locker? That will leave our hands free to buy what's left on our lists."

We pushed ourselves hard and fast and crossed off almost everything we'd written down. I had a Christmas present for each person in the house.

We wound up the day with a marvelous, though rather late, lunch. John ordered a lovely rose' wine to go with our quiche Lorraine. We finished the meal with coffee and devoured delectable raspberry tarts. John claimed our packages from the lockers and almost missed the train. When the engine lurched forward, he tumbled up the steps of the train car. There was clank of passenger cars on the rails and he staggered down the aisle and into our compartment. The train gave a jerk and he landed on top of me. When we got our breath back we began to laugh, and I know the two elderly ladies who shared our section thought us blatantly indecent.

As we untangled ourselves it crossed my mind that I liked it when John and I were close, touching, that is. He smelled of a lemony soap and the scent intrigued me. I also enjoyed those chaste kisses he occasionally bestowed on my cheek.

I took a note pad out of my purse and we reviewed our purchases. Before long we started a new list. "You know, John, we'll never ever get everything bought for the house. I hope we receive a pile of catalogs from the British supply houses soon. We can't run off to the city every week to buy the odd little items we need for the rooms."

"You're right about that. Listen, when can we realistically open our doors as a B-and-B? Let's set a tentative date. How about March 1?"

"That sounds fine to me. We probably don't need that long but I'd rather start slow. If someone knocks on our door sooner, we can let them come in and we'll experiment on them."

John laughed. "You mean experiment like try out new recipes for mulberry scones or did you have something more sinister in mind?"

He made me laugh. "Take your choice, but I also thought about trying out our roles as hosts. Who's going to do the check-in? Who will carry their bags and show them to their rooms?"

"I figured Harry would do the bags. You can give them our new brochure with the map of the house and let them find their way up to the rooms."

"And what will you be doing, Mr. Fordyce? Surely you have a place in the overall scheme besides being the person who pays the bills and keeps the books."

"Oh, there are lots of things I can do. After tea I'll be the bartender while you help clear up the dirty dishes."

I couldn't help snorting at him. "It's so kind of you to include me in the activities, sir. I'd feel left out if there weren't any chores for me. I expect as we work into the business we'll each find our level and also help out by filling in wherever we're needed."

"Righto. Better gather your packages and be ready to jump off the train. We're pulling into the station right now."

Harry came to meet us. How good it felt to sit squashed in the lorry and drive up the long lane to Hollystone. The house radiated heat from a fire in the great hall and the tea tray waited with fairy cakes and tomato-cheese sandwiches. The entire household gathered in the morning room to hear about our trip, including baby Jamie.

Lady Sheila poured out the tea and I took a sip from my cup. "We stayed at both ends of the scale. The first night my room was awful and the breakfast tasted worse. John fared better. And so did I last night when I stayed in a much nicer place. I doubt John even saw his room because the shopping exhausted him. Do you remember enough to give us a report?"

"After a good sleep, I found my second night's lodging to be mediocre at best. Hollystone is going to be a classy place compared to the hotels we stayed in. If we can just get people to come, we'll have a gold mine here."

I carried a few of the small shampoo and lotion containers to show the others. Lady Sheila reached for one of the little bottles. "These are so clever, Glennie. The wee crown lids will add a touch of class to the baths. Oh, and I do like the gold baskets to hold them."

Ellen sniffed and clutched Jamie against her flat bosom. "Looks too fancy to me. You'll be after overcharging folks to pay for all those extras."

I couldn't resist stirring the pot and riling Ellen a bit more. "You should see the decorative candies we've ordered to put on the guests' pillows at bedtime. They're chocolate mints with a holly design on them. The package will have a sprig of holly on it also." This produced a big sniff from Ellen, who took Jamie off to his crib.

CHAPTER 19

We backed off on the bed-and-breakfast as Christmas came rushing down on us. Ellen and Lady Sheila insisted on a tree. "We must have one for Jamie's first yuletide." John and Harry went out to the acres of woods belonging to the estate and dragged home a gem of a tree. It stood tall and fat and they set it up in the hall to the right of the fireplace. I'd purchased decorations while in London and John helped me cover the tree with tiny white lights. We added red balls and silver trinkets to dress it up.

The first time we showed Jamie the tree, his brown eyes glowed. Ellen said, "Whist, he can't see the pretties yet. Wait until next year when he can run around and grab the shiny balls. Then we'll have our hands full."

I spent a morning cutting holly sprays from the bushes that surrounded the house. When great bunches of them were arranged in antique brass containers they looked wonderful in the hall, if I do say so. Presents began to appear around the tree and I heard much whispering and rustling of paper wrappings.

At lunch a few days before the big day I looked around the table. "Jilly and I need a count of who will be here for Christmas dinner and other holiday meals."

Lady Sheila spoke up first. "Guy called last evening and said he'll fly in on the twenty-fourth for a brief visit. Ellen and I will be here. Also, Guy's brother Ransome called and will join us. Glennie, have you any plans?"

"No, ma'am, nary a plan. John, what about you?"

103

"My mum wrote that she'd like to come for a few days. Is that all right, Lady Sheila?"

"You know it's fine, John, and what's with this lady business? You used to call me Aunt Sheila."

"I know, but since everyone else calls you 'lady,' I just do too. I think that when we have guests it would be best to do it that way. Maybe I can remember to say Auntie when we're alone."

"Very well, John. I look forward to seeing Mayme Fordyce. Your mother and I are great friends. Of course she wears me out, but I'll have plenty of time to rest between chats."

When I quizzed Harry and Jilly about their families, only Jilly's father planned to join us. The others felt their visit for the Burn's wedding and Jamie's christening was enough travel for the year.

The hustle and bustle of Christmas got into high gear. John must have wired his mother that same day because she arrived on the evening train twenty-four hours later. Mayme Fordyce had a stocky build, but wasn't a fat woman. It was easy to see where John got his brown eyes and dark curls. Her hair showed a bit of gray, but she looked quite young. I couldn't believe she and Lady Sheila were contemporaries. This woman was vigorous, hearty, bossy, and talkative.

Her first words to me were, "Hello, Glenna James. I've heard lots about you. Most all of it good. I think John's sweet on you from the way he blushes at the mention of your name." He immediately turned brick red and so did I. We left her having tea in the parlor with Lady Sheila and he turned to me and began to apologize.

I held up my hand to stop him. "Don't say it. She's a twin to my mother. If I don't mind what your mother says, you can forget my pushy parents. Let's simply ignore her comments. We can change the subject any time she comes out with one of her pointed remarks. We'll deal with her as a team and gang up on her."

"You're brilliant, Glennie.

With a shake of my head I said, "No, I've had more practice. You've spent over half your life away at school while I lived at home until I went to college. Even then I wasn't allowed to get too far away. You can't imagine the uproar when I bought my house and actually lived there alone."

John gave me a knowing look. "Having met your parents I can imagine that put the cat among the pigeons."

It turned out to be a blessed Christmas. After a supper of oyster stew and holiday cookies, we all, except Ellen and Jamie, went to eleven o'clock services in the village Kirk on Christmas Eve. The next morning we slept in and gathered around the tree about ten o'clock for tea and Jilly's cinnamon buns.

Harry built a roaring blaze in the fireplace and Jilly's jolly pa handed around the tea. "And a Merry Christmas to you," he said as he gave us each our cup.

We expected Guy the evening before but he blew in the door just in time to stuff one of the cinnamon rolls in his mouth. He seemed to exude the spicy fragrances of the Far East, where he'd just come from. The taxi driver helped him haul in a load of packages. Some of them were in huge boxes and they certainly swelled the display under the tree. He happened to run into his brother, Ransome, at the airport and brought him along in the taxi.

Ransome looked a great deal like Guy except he was several inches shorter. He had the same blond hair and blue eyes, but his chin looked a bit weak. He made a fuss over his mother and had a few words with his Aunt Mayme. At the first opportunity John took me aside. "Don't let Ransome get you alone. He's been in a spot of trouble before for roughing up girls. He and the drink don't mix well."

We had agreed to open gifts after breakfast and as soon as Jilly and I cleared up we gathered around the tree. Even at my stage in life I began to feel a bubble of excitement rise in my chest. I wanted to know what was hidden in some of those fancy boxes and I hoped everyone would like what I chose for them. Lady Sheila and Ellen seemed pleased with the shawl and purse. Mrs. Fordyce thanked me nicely for the silk scarf I'd snatched from a village shop at the last minute. She immediately went to a mirror and tied it around her neck.

Jamie made a huge haul. Guy produced an enormous hobbyhorse and I swear the child will not be able to climb up on his steed till he's ready for kindergarten. John sensibly presented him with a large box of blocks, which the baby chewed on with approval. John and I had purchased the baby bed when we shopped in London and it brought tears to Jilly's eyes.

"Oh, John and Glennie, you've been so good to us and now this wonderful bed. We thank you more than you know. I've been putting a bit by each week from our pay, but I worried Jamie would outgrow the basket long before we had enough."

Guy dragged a box the size of a coffin up to me and out of the wrapping came a magnificent carved wooden chest. It was beautiful. Guy's eyes were watchful as he tried to get a feel for my reaction to his offering. "I'm overwhelmed. It's beautiful and smells of all the spices of the orient. Is it sandalwood?"

"You guessed right; it came from China."

"Mother will be thrilled. She's been after me to start a hope chest for years now." Everyone laughed, which was the response I wanted.

Later when John and I set the dining room table for dinner, he reached in his pocket and handed me a tiny package. "I wanted to give this to you privately," he said.

I slipped the ribbon off, lifted the lid, and found a pair of pearl earrings. They stunned me, left me absolutely flabbergasted. I first thought they couldn't be real. But as I read the information on the box it became obvious they were valuable pieces of jewelry. He had no reason to present me with a gift of that magnitude. "John, you can't give me a present like this. This is too much, I can't accept the pearls."

He gave me a most serious look. "Yes, Glennie, you can accept them. There are no strings attached. You've been wonderful to work with and I consider you one of my best friends. Now as friend-to-friend you must put them in your ears and enjoy them. And thank you for the handsome wristwatch you gave me. As you know, I needed one. And I realize you've given me a rather special timepiece. It's great to be able to see what time it is in Hong Kong."

This time John changed tactics and gave me a light kiss on the lips. Why did that butterfly touch of a kiss make me tingle all over? I didn't know the answer and later I thought about it but not long enough. I should have realized then what was happening to John and me.

Jilly's Christmas goose with all the fixings made a grand holiday dinner. We did as folks the world over do; we ate too much. Every one of us slipped off for a snooze when the remains of the meal were in the refrigerator and the dishes sudsing away in the machine. Never was I as thankful for the new dishwasher as I was that day.

About seven o'clock that evening I woke and dragged myself out of bed. I washed my face to help me wake up and reapplied my lipstick. I found Jilly down in the kitchen making sliced goose sandwiches. I took the leftover cranberry salad out of the fridge and we set out a buffet for supper. No one had saved room for dessert after dinner so my chocolate-mint delight would finish off our evening meal. I'd concocted the dessert with a chocolate-cookie crust, lots of whipped cream, marshmallows, and crème de menthe liqueur. John's mother raved about it and there was precious little left at the end of our meal.

We had a festive time with Jilly's dad, Bill Warrick, he being a most entertaining man. Wonder of wonders, he and Mayme Fordyce seemed to enjoy each other immensely. Bill's eyes twinkled as he sat by the fire with Jamie on his lap. "And so you're down from Scotland for the holidays. When will you be going back to that snowy place?"

"I probably won't return. The cold and snow make my hips ache. I may stay in this warm, comfy house with my son."

John sent a surprised look her way. "That's news to me, Mum. Are you really wanting to stay here?"

"If you'll have me, son."

Just like that, Mayme Fordyce became a part of the Hollystone family and I found her delightful.

When Jamie became fussy, Jilly took him off to bed and we could feel the day winding down. We turned into a mellow group and after Guy got out the brandy bottle we were practically comatose. I rank it as one of the best Christmases I ever spent.

CHAPTER 20

The next day we enjoyed Boxing Day, a British holiday I didn't know anything about. We lazed around and ate leftovers. After lunch Guy invited me to go for a walk on the grounds. I grabbed my coat and met him in the great hall. As he helped me put on my jacket I wondered what he wanted to talk about.

"Glenna, tell me how things are going for you."

"No big problems. Everyone gets along well. I'm sure we'll be ready to open on March first or even earlier. There's plenty of work to finish up but neither John nor I see any thing ahead that we can't deal with."

"Good. You two make a great team. I'm so glad I hired you. You can do anything, can't you?"

I shoved my hands in my pockets and looked up at him. "Thank you for your kind words, sir."

"So, do you have plans for your future, Glenna? Are you thinking of marriage? Do you want to settle down?"

This fellow was something else. Why couldn't he say what was on his mind? "Surely you know I don't have any designs on the future, only the usual hopes and dreams. After you met my parents you must realize that I've spent a great many years shying away from commitments."

"I'm sorry I haven't called you or sent e-mails. When I get busy, I forget everything else. There is nothing so demanding or as exciting as an oil well about to come in. I do manage to call Mother fairly often. Does she give you my messages?"

"She's given me some. Nothing personal though. Sometimes I wonder where our relationship's going. I'm in no hurry but all women my age begin to worry about their biological clocks. That means I don't want to wait to have kids until I'm forty or older. I know I've resisted commitments partly because it's become so important to my parents, but it would be foolish to lose out altogether just to spite them. We call that throwing the baby out with the bathwater."

Guy laughed out loud. "What a wonderful way you have of explaining things." Then he spoke more soberly. "I've been giving the future a great deal of thought. I'm trying to see what direction my business will go and whether I can stop this ceaseless race around the globe. I'll likely miss the excitement of travel if I give it up. What do you think about my lifestyle? Does it seem foolish to you?"

"I look at maturity as making sensible decisions and possibly giving up a few things in a trade for stability and security."

He shrugged his shoulders. "That's what worries me. How does one know when it's time to be sensible? I feel as if I'm on a race track and I'm afraid to jump off while my horse is going around."

"I hope you can come to terms with your life, Guy. Many men would envy you your freedom, but others would find it a dreary treadmill. Only you can decide what works for you." There, I had my say but left the door open for the future. That's the best I could do. He seemed fearful to commit himself to making changes in his life. He could have suggested I travel with him. He left me with one of his special kisses, but the electricity seemed to be on low voltage.

John drove Guy to the airport and I had no regrets as I watched him leave. It seemed almost like a non-event compared to the feelings I'd experienced earlier. Things were changing but I didn't know where my life was headed.

The following day we dived into the final plans and arrangements for Hollystone House. I checked with the Jardine boys, since they were local, as to whom we could hire as room maids. Mick immediately jumped at the opportunity. "I reckon my ole missus could do the job. Her liked it when you had she over to clean before her Ladyship come and her been talking about takin' on some work. Her were right set up to clean in a big house like Hollystone."

Rick had to add his bit. "My missus might like a bit of a job, now the kids be grown and away. Her sister do cleanin' work and they both might want to tackle the job. Shall I have them call round to talk with you, Miss Glennie?"

"Yes, please ask all three women to come see me. We'll probably need more than just the guest rooms done up regularly. Could they come tomorrow morning about ten? Tell them we'll have a cup of tea and talk things over."

I could hear Mick speak to Rick as I walked out of the room. "That Miss Glennie is orl right. Not many ladies hiring maids would offer them tea."

I'd only met the Jardine women at Jilly and Harry's wedding and when they'd cleaned Lady Sheila's rooms, but I recognized them when the came to the house. Betty and Mabel were definitely sisters, with their brown hair streaked with gray and screwed up in tight perms. Jean, a faded blonde, kept very quiet. All three were a bit heavy and wore starched, cotton housedresses.

Jilly, busy trying new cookie and teacake recipes, brought up a plate of samples. Not only did I offer tea, but also had biscuits, which are still cookies to me. The three women, seated around the table in the morning room, each clutched a teacup. We talked in generalities at first. Then I topped off their cups and passed the cookie plate again. "We want the rooms and hallways to be extra clean. People remember things like gritty floors and might not come back." They agreed that extreme cleanliness should be their goal.

In the end Mabel and Jean would do up the rooms and Betty would clean the great hall, the common rooms, and the kitchen. They would trade around to cover weekends so each would have two days off a week. Also, they would take care of the laundry. I agreed to their wage requests and they seemed quite pleased. I felt relieved to cross that responsibility off my list.

Before they left, I wanted their opinions on the pastries. "Now which one of these biscuits do you like best? We have to decide what we'll be serving the inn guests." They disagreed as to their favorites, and I reported the mixed results to Jilly. Actually I liked them all.

After a lunch of tiny sandwiches (all our meals these days were tryouts for future guests), I asked John to join me in the dining room/ office. "We have to get the great hall sorted out. We need a bar, a TV corner, and a check-in desk. How can we arrange all those things without having a room full of clutter?"

"How about if we put the telly at a ninety-degree angle to the fireplace? Then put rockers and comfortable sofas around so guests can enjoy a nice fire and the news at the same time."

"Do we really want the TV by the fireplace? Somehow I can see the women clustered about the fire chatting away and the men settled in another corner to watch a soccer game."

"That probably makes more sense. Are we going to use the parlor or lounge for anything? You have it decorated so beautifully and I rather hate to let people just wear it out."

"If we can possibly avoid it, let's not use that room. Maybe some evening in the future we'll have a musicale and it would be super for that. But we won't allow guests to eat food in there. That would ruin the carpet quicker than anything. I know Lady Sheila and your mother like to have tea in that room, but they are quite careful not to spill crumbs. The hall is huge and we should be able to fit in everything we need."

By dinnertime we'd hammered out a workable plan. The west wall had the enormous fireplace and we would cluster plushy furniture around it for visiting. Seating needed to be purchased, as we were using leftovers from the forties that showed signs of age. A spring would occasionally poke up through a seat cushions and give one of us a jab.

I put a call into Harrods and ordered the furniture. It would be leather in a port wine color. Two sofas and six chairs duly arrived, after we arranged for custom wheels to be fitted underneath. That way we could easily shove the seating around for maximum comfort.

Twenty feet back from the double front doors on the east, we placed a large desk and a couple of chairs. Guests would check in there. On the north wall we elevated a big screen TV that could be seen from most of the hall. Below the television we placed an antique bar that Mick Jardine put us onto.

The day after Mick mentioned the bar, John came into the room where I stuffed some velvet pillows into shams for the new sofa. "Let's go take a look at the old bar. Mick told me how to find it. I'll treat you to a lunch while we're out."

"I haven't had a better offer today. Let's go."

We drove to Chartwell, the next village, and John pulled into a real razzle-dazzle-looking nightclub. In fact the owners named it the "Razzle-Dazzle." The place glowed with neon lights inside and out. John tracked down the owner, and brought him back to the ladies' bar where I waited.

"Miss Glenna James, this is Mr. Adamson that the Jardines told us about."

Mr. Adamson looked elderly and a bit shaky, but his steely-blue eyes beamed as bright as headlights. "How do, miss. Mister here says ye want to take a peep at me old bar. It's out behind if ye'll just follow me."

We crowded into a little shed and there it stood. The gorgeous black oak bar just bowled me over with its carving. The back bar leaning against the wall gleamed with mirrors. I knew I should have kept still but I couldn't help but say, "Oh, John, it's beautiful. We've got to have it."

He gave me a quelling frown and turned to the owner. "How much ye askin' for it, Mr. Adamson?" It amused me that when John was stressed or about to do a deal his vocabulary included more Scottish words and expressions.

Mr. Adamson kicked the ground for a while and finally named a price. John shot me a glance that said *look what you've done*.

Now I was treated to a demonstration of how a canny Scot makes a deal. John folded his arms and just stared at the bar. Then he ran his hand over the surface and shook his head.

When I almost screamed to break the silence, he finally spoke. "I'll gie ye half if ye'll throw in them bar stools."

Now Mr. Adamson took a turn to ponder the deal silently. He stood on one foot and then the other. He shook his head after a while. When he at last spoke, he hit below the belt. "Mother, she sets great store on that bar. Her cried the day Mick and Rick yanked it out and installed the new one." More silence followed. John showed great willpower because at last Mr. Adamson appeared to make a decision. "I'll split the difference with ye, young man."

More staring into space and floor kicking followed. When I truly thought I would run shrieking from the shed John frowned. "Aye, we'll do er' if ye'll throw in that dusty old mirror in the corner."

After a brief pause Mr. Adamson thrust out his hand to John. "Ye've got a deal, laddie."

I almost fainted with relief.

We crowded into the wee office where John wrote a check. We drank a thimbleful of sherry and shook hands all around. John and I then repaired to an old drinking bar on the edge of Chartwell for our lunch of pub grub.

"I must say, Glenna, the next time we go out buying antique bars, it would be best if you kept your mouth tightly shut."

"I'm sorry. It's just so beautiful I couldn't help but exclaim. I know better. Really I do. I used to bargain for antiques back home when I shopped for clients. What interests me is how you lapsed into broad Scots for your haggling. Did you realize it?"

"Of course I did. The old man came from up near Ballydendron and I knew he'd be kinder to a fellow from home."

"Well, how do we get the monster bar back to Hollystone?"

"I think the Jardines have a bigger truck. I'll ask them to fetch it. Now have you had enough fish and chips? If so, we better get back and finish furnishing our hall."

That afternoon we unpacked several sets of bridge tables with folding chairs and placed them in the area of the south wall between the library and morning room doors. They were to be multi-purpose. Folks could play cards or put puzzles together there. In the mornings they'd enjoy their gourmet breakfasts at the tables and have tea there in the late afternoon.

The handsome oak staircase had its place in the northwest corner of the great hall. Under it a passage way led to the butler's pantry, which became the phone and modem room. I found some black and white wallpaper that featured those round, red, pay phone boxes that are so typical of a somewhat earlier English landscape. The Jardine boys wired in the modem hookups. Small black tables and chairs completed the room and I loved it.

A guest loo and cloakroom were created out of a seldom-used bathroom and storage area between the library and the morning room. While we planned, changed our minds, and made final decisions, Ransome got under our feet almost constantly. He tried to be charming, but I found myself feeling quite annoyed with him. As soon as I placed a chair in front of the fireplace, he'd move it.

John finally suggested that he run some errands for us, an assignment that appealed to him as it included the keys to the truck. He invited me to go with him and proposed we stay out for lunch. "After all, Glenna, I've had about all the tea sandwiches I can stand instead of regular meals."

"I don't think so, Ransome. I have a great deal of work to do and can't take the time to run all over the countryside." He tried to hit on me at least three times a day. I sensed something about him that seemed slightly evil and it made me uneasy. To quote my oldest newphew, "He creeped me out."

In the midst of an orgy of organizing and setting up, Lady Sheila came to me and asked for a job. "I can surely do something, Glenna. Could I check in the guests? I've seen your brochures with maps of the house in them. In the morning I could organize a little packet for each person or couple. I'd check to see which rooms you assigned to the guests and mark it on the maps. The key could be in the packet too. Then I would ask their interests and give them little handouts about the local sights worth seeing."

She looked so eager that I barely hesitated before saying yes. If she became too worn-out, I could take the work back since I'd planned to do the job myself. I didn't question but that she'd add a touch of class to our operation. Welcoming our visitors in her navy or black dresses with the white lace collars and cuffs would certainly impress the them.

Harry and John put up the elegant sign Harry designed and painted for us. He'd lettered in gold over red and it stood out beautifully with the sprigs of holly painted around the words.

CHAPTER 21

The final struggle surfaced over who would work what hours. It began to look as if we'd need more people to get the job done. I remained adamant that we all needed days off. We'd worked seven days a week while we decorated and set up the place, but now that the time had come to operate a business, we must be professional. People who had no days off would soon get cranky and out of sorts. Nothing would get us off on the wrong foot faster than unhappy employees, me included.

I posted a schedule in the morning room and, as she wished, included Lady Sheila. Actually, if it worked out for her to check the guests in, it would help me a great deal. I would have that time of day to rest, or on Jilly's days off I could put the tea together. John would be backup and carry luggage for the guests on Harry's free days.

It occurred to me that we should include Ransome on the work roster. He certainly did nothing now but get in our way and give me the eye. His one job of running errands ended with his returning late that night with a dent in the truck fender. John and I privately agreed to hide the truck keys and not allow Ransome to drive. When we sat down for a quick tea break, I made a suggestion. "Why don't we make a bartender out of him?"

"Oh no, Glennie. Maybe you haven't noticed that Ransome has a wee problem with the drink. In fact, one of my jobs is to try and keep him out of the bottles. I've locked up the liquor all the time he's been here and I'll only unlock it when there are guests to serve or one of us wants a drink. Now he could carry luggage in for the guests, but my hunch is he'll disappear as soon as the first car comes up the drive."

"He's just about worthless, isn't he?"

He bit into a biscuit. "I wish we could give him the boot but it would hurt Lady Sheila. She feels responsible for his shortcomings because she became quite ill when he was a child. She always thought his father sent him off to boarding school too young and blamed herself for his problems. And his father, my Uncle George, died rather young and she believes that affected him too. Personally, I think he was born rotten clear through. Guy grew up in the same environment and he isn't like Ransome at all."

"What does he live on if he doesn't work?"

"Guy makes him a small allowance. It never lasts from quarter to quarter so he has to come home to live until the next installment. That's why he's here now. Don't lend him any money because you'll never see a farthing of it back. I'm sure he's only here till his next quarter stipend comes due."

John's mother definitely elected to stay on with us for a time. She really did annoy him but I liked her. She didn't interfere with our work or plans but spent time with Lady Sheila. They had long discussions while they worked on embroidery and knitting. After a session Lady Sheila would sneak into her room for a rest and I would know Mayme Fordyce had worn her out one more time."

John spent a couple of mornings with Lady Sheila, to teach her the check-in procedure. He showed her how to use the credit card machine. That, he pointed out, was the most important part of her job. Get that card imprint and or collect the cash or check.

I began to feel real excitement the day the ads appeared. The men planted the sign outside the main gate, the little shampoo bottles with the gold crown tops nestled in their gold baskets. Jilly had the freezer full of her scrumptious baked good and the inn was ready for breakfast. We always had something we needed to do but essentially we were ready. For about a week we waited for that first phone call and when nothing happened we began to get edgy.

One evening John and I were on the verge of hurtling teacups at each other. "Glennie, let's get out of here. I have cabin fever. Why don't we visit the pub in the village and have a beer. We need to see some different people and get out of our rut."

"You're right. Can we invite Harry and Jilly along? They have even less social life than you and I do."

"Sure, round them up. Old Ellen can listen for Jamie and we'll go out and have a bang-up time at the Crown and Anchor. Don't let Ransome know we're going. We don't need him getting violent after several drinks."

The Burnses were thrilled to have an evening on the town. Ellen agreed to watch the baby, but you could tell she didn't approve of such nonsense as ladies visiting the pub. We alerted Lady Sheila to answer the phone and take messages. After a flurry of activity the four of us piled into the Land Rover, which was sized for about two and a half people. But we cared not a bit. We were starved for any kind of social life.

The Crown and Anchor Pub looked typical of the genre, with dark, almost black, wood paneling. It had a fruity smell from the gallons of brew that customers had spilled on its floors, tables, and counters over the centuries. The cigarette smoke that swirled around the room made the place seem friendly and welcoming. Any other day I would detest the smoke and odors, but tonight I wanted to enjoy the whole scene.

We settled at a table and the middle-aged barmaid delivered the first of what turned out to be too many drinks. We acted like kids let out of school. Quiet Harry began to tell jokes that made us convulse with laughter. Fortunately most of the locals stayed at home this particular evening. Otherwise we would've ruined the reputation of "them that lives up to the big house."

When John bought a round for the house, the handful of other patrons gathered around and told a few jokes of their own. Before long we were all the best of friends. I can't recall when I have enjoyed as much silly fun as I did that night. At midnight most of the other customers headed for their homes and we, with our fuzzy headed lack of sense, decided we should take off as well. We were not too far-gone to know that some of us were not fit to drive home. Jilly had stuck with soft drinks because of nursing Jamie. We elected her as the obvious choice to chauffeur us home. She threw up her hands. "But I can't drive. I've never had a chance to learn."

Harry stood swaying by the door. "Doesn't matter, It's better you drive than one of us."

"But I can't," she said again. "I could get arrested by the constable and I don't have a license."

Then clever John had an idea. "Jilly, steer with the wheel. I'll run the gearshift and the brake."

I had to get my two cents in. "Who'll tell her when to turn right or left?"

John and Harry both said, "Never mind that." John climbed into the driver's seat. "Come on, Jilly. Slide under the wheel and sit here on my lap. Now I'll turn the key on and get her started. You hang onto the wheel and steer. I'll work the pedals."

Jilly became panic-stricken and steered us down a ditch and across someone's yard, leaving noticeable ruts. Somehow Harry ended up on my lap and even though his body was skinny as a toothpick he seemed to weigh a ton.

After several false starts we made it up the long drive to the house. The final stop ended with the front wheels in a thicket of holly bushes. We piled out and every one shushed everyone else. Jilly got the front door open and we straggled in to find Lady Sheila asleep in front of the fireplace.

She roused up immediately since our shushing and giggles echoed around the hall. "Well, there you are, children." She emphasized children. "I have good news. Our first guests are on the second floor asleep, while visions of breakfast cinnamon buns dance in their heads."

Some of us sobered up swiftly. Harry collapsed onto a chair and fell sound asleep. Jilly put a hand over her mouth and looked horrified. Breakfast was her job and she had nothing ready. She ran for the kitchen and we could hear her bang pots and pans as she pulled together a couple of quick dishes for morning.

Lady Sheila went on to tell us about our visitors. "These two American couples were on their way down from Scotland by auto when a breakdown stranded them here. Someone directed them to the Central Lodging Office in town. Those folks called us and I said we certainly could take them. You'll find their registration on the desk with the credit card verification attached. I believe everything is in order and I'm going to bed."

John and I looked at each other. Rarely have I felt as embarrassed as I did that night. He raised one eyebrow at me. "Boys will be boys and I guess girls will get carried away too. Can I give you a hand up the stairs?"

He put an arm around my shoulders and we kept each other steady as we climbed upward. It turned into a long slow trip as we'd moved to the fourth floor during the final stages of preparing the guest rooms. We'd ripped out some walls and made ourselves decent suites. We paused at my door, which John opened. He guided me in and said good night with one of his soft, sweet kisses. I had begun to look forward to them. They were so warm. Yes, warm was the word. Sometime I would like to explore them more fully but not tonight. Before I fell asleep I set the alarm for 6:00 a.m.

CHAPTER 22

When the alarm went off at that ungodly early hour I cursed my behavior of the night before, but managed to drag myself into the shower and wake up enough to dress and swallow a couple of aspirin. I sped down the stairs to the kitchen. I would have given a lot to have the lift available. The men would come to install it in another two weeks.

I relaxed in the kitchen when I saw that Jilly had pulled things together last night. A pan of her delectable cinnamon rolls had risen and looked about ready to go into the oven. In the fridge an egg-sausage casserole waited its turn in the stove, so I turned on the oven. She'd filled the new coffeemaker and it looked ready to do its job, as did the electric teakettle. I began to chop bananas and oranges for a fruit cup.

The dishes were stacked neatly with napkins and silverware so I lugged the tray to the first floor and began to set up the bridge tables. Then I took everything off again as I realized we must use tablecloths or place mats.

I found the new tablecloths in the Welch dresser and started over again. The headache that ground away behind my eyes got worse and I had to stop and climb all the way to the fourth floor for two more aspirin. I vowed that never again would I overindulge as I had the evening before.

By the time I reset the table John appeared. His bloodshot eyes attested to the fact that he felt no better than I did. "It's all ready to go. Jilly must have stayed up till three o'clock to get the food prepared. I don't know whether she'll be down in time to put the dishes in the oven or not."

John wisely turned on the electric kettle and brewed tea while I shoved the rolls into the oven. We sat quietly in the kitchen and drank an entire pot of the magic drink. Finally I could string a few words together. "How's your cabin fever doing, John? Did the alcoholic cure work?"

"Don't make me laugh. My head won't stand it. I should have stayed with the beer." He put his head in his hands and sighed heavily.

Jilly rushed in, handed baby Jamie to me, and took over the kitchen work. When the guests appeared about eight, they never knew how lucky they were to have a delicious breakfast. Jilly served neatly and charmed the folks with her soft Yorkshire accent. John and I feasted on leftover cinnamon buns and I privately said prayers of thankfulness that it had all gone so well.

Later that morning Ransome made a dramatic entrance and threw a huge tantrum, aiming his attack at John. "You're just rotten to have gone off without me last night. You know I don't have a car and you left me here with the old ladies. Tonight I'm going to take the keys to the truck and go out on my own."

I looked at John with a raised eyebrow. He nodded to indicate that he'd hide the truck keys extra carefully. Lady Sheila drifted into the great hall and Ransome shut up fast enough. God, he must embarrass her.

I could not resist prodding him. "I'm so glad you were home last night to carry the guests' bags up to their rooms. You'll be around to bring them down again, won't you?"

He muttered, "Sure," and disappeared in a hurry.

After our rocky start in the lodging business, we were deluged with people who clamored for our guest rooms. I was busy day after day with reservations. So much so in fact that we realized we could rent more rooms than we had available. After a hasty consultation, John tracked Guy down in Alaska and received his go-ahead to start work on the rest of the fourth floor.

We called the Jardine brothers and set them to work with Harry on the old servants' quarters. By converting the small cribs into larger areas we could add about six more units. Plus they made improvements in John's and my rooms by adding private baths. When they finished the work Jilly and Harry would have a four-room apartment in the north wing. We let them do the decorating and they chose ivory walls and pale-cream furniture. Then they added pictures, pillows, rugs, and pottery pieces in bright primary colors. The rooms looked cheerful and warm.

For John's room I picked a brown, black, and cream plaid carpet. Harry painted one wall ivory, the second wall taupe, and the third wall chocolate. He striped the fourth wall in the three colors. The two windows were in the ivory wall and cream Hessian draperies covered them.

I found a bedcover in a cream, brown, and ebony paisley design and with the addition of three steel engravings from the attic, the room looked very masculine. Oh, yes, a red blanket lay folded at the foot of the bed and I tossed two red and black pillows on the spread.

We did up my room in light blues, greens, and a touch of purple. After installing a comfortable chair and a reading lamp I moved into my snug retreat.

Ransome constantly got under foot and demanded one of the new large rooms. "I'm tired of sleeping on the divan in Mother's sitting room. I need my own place."

John finally had to tell him off. "If you don't take yourself out of the workmen's way, I'm going to call Guy and have your allowance cut off." The boy huffed around for several days and then disappeared for a week. While he was away, John told me more about him. "A couple of years ago Ransome roughed up a girl in Scotland. Guy paid her father a large sum of money because of the damage the fool did. He broke the poor lass's arm and scarred her face. He works himself into uncontrollable rages and then, look out."

"My heavens, he's dangerous!"

"Only when he gets into the drink. Otherwise he's simply annoying."

We were too busy to miss him. I hired a girl, Elspeth, to help Jilly in the kitchen. We also added another maid, Jean Jardine's cousin Clara, to keep up with the work.

One evening after an especially busy day I shut down my computer and rode the new lift to the fourth floor. As I stepped out into the dark hallway someone grabbed me, slapped a hand over my mouth, and dragged me into my room. A strong smell of liquor invaded the room and I barely made out Ransome's features in the dim light. He flung me onto the bed, tore off a strip of furnace tape, and placed it tightly over my mouth.

I was furious and fought like a tiger, so he couldn't hold me down long enough to tape my wrists to the bedposts. That in no way discouraged him though, just made him angry. He decided to skip that step and began to pull at my clothes. I continued to fight and make as much noise as possible. I flung myself off the bed and onto the floor. What a relief to hear the elevator stop on the fourth floor. I kicked the room door continually and heard Harry call out. "Glennie, are you okay?"

Ransome flipped the lock closed and tried to drag me back toward the bed. I fought him wildly and kept kicking the door. He tried to kneel on my legs and stop me. My frantic efforts made so much noise that Harry hurried to find John and a master key.

Ransome began to rave. "Glennie, you go around here so stuck-up, acting high and mighty, as if you're too good for me. Well, I'm going to show you I'm as good as Guy or John." When I heard a key turn in the lock I let out a big breath of relief as the two men burst into the room. Harry took hold of Ransome and hauled him to his feet. John slugged him in the face repeatedly until his nose and mouth looked like jelly. They dragged him into the hall, shoved him into an unfinished bathroom, and locked him away.

John lifted me off the floor and laid me on the bed. Harry yanked the adhesive patch off my mouth with a bit too much vigor and a bit of skin came with the tape. Jilly came out of their apartment. "What's all this fuss about? Oh, my word. Glennie, are you hurt? What happened?" When she saw my face she ran for the Vaseline and began to spread it on my lips and the surrounding skin.

"What on earth did Ransome do to you?" John asked. "Tell me, Glenna, are you hurt?"

I felt so enraged I could barely talk about the attack. I had a pretty good idea what had caused Ransome to treat me so brutally. "Ransome's drunk. He waited for me when I got off the elevator. He had the tape cut and ready to use. See, there are the other pieces stuck to the bedpost so he could bind my wrists." John pulled the tape free with an angry yank. After balling it up, he flung the wad out in the hallway.

"I fought so hard he couldn't get a hold of my arms and then Harry heard me kicking the door and went for you, John. Ransome locked the door so no one could get in—." With that I ran out of words. The fight had worn me out and my back hurt from my tumble off the bed. Tears dripped down my cheeks, which caused John to hover over me, patting my hand.

John's mother, Mayme, burst through the door with her curly hair standing on end. "I could hear you clear down on second. You'll have the guests awake and out in the hall asking questions. Now what on earth's happened?"

Harry and John gave her a sketchy account of Ransome's attack on me. Her face flushed with indignation. "I never heard of such a thing. He'll have to go in the morning. Sheila can't want him here after what's happened. Where is he now?"

John gestured toward the hall. "He's sleeping it off in one of the new bathrooms. He's locked in and I suggest we leave him there till morning. Then I'll personally escort him off the premises. Let's make Glenna comfortable for the night. Mother, will you help her out of her clothes and get her settled?"

"Yes, I certainly will. The rest of you go on to bed. Oh, John, could you get some ice from that new machine in your bar? I think it would feel good on Glennie's face and her foot. Put it in some plastic bags. Better bring her a glass of ice water too. I'm sure her mouth needs rinsing after being taped shut."

Mayme treated me with great tenderness. Before she took my torn clothes off, she headed for my closet. "Where's your nightie, dear?"

"It's not really a nightie, ma'am. You'll find an large T-shirt hanging on a hook. That's what I usually sleep in." She hid her shock at such a thing and carefully pulled it over my head.

"Do you want to visit the loo? I almost forgot that."

"No, I used the one downstairs just before I came up in the lift. I'll be fine after John gets here with my drink."

He walked in then with the water, an ice pack, and two Ibuprofen. He lifted my head and helped me take the pills. After he placed the ice over my mouth he dropped a kiss on my forehead and gave his mother a hug. "Goodnight, Glennie. Hope you can sleep. And don't worry, Ransome is locked in the bathroom and he can't get to you again. Tomorrow he gets the boot."

Mayme looked slyly at me when he'd gone. "He's a good fellow, you know. Salt of the earth like his father." With that she left me to doze off, which I did more quickly than I expected.

CHAPTER 23

I slept through the night, woke about seven, and needed to visit the loo urgently. I sat up and decided I was pretty much okay after my ordeal. After a minute I stood and took one step toward the closet for my robe. I discovered immediately that I could go no farther. Something felt terribly wrong with my right foot. I couldn't imagine what had happened, but there was no way that foot would bear my weight. I tried to hop to the bathroom, but the jump up and down caused my foot to throb unbearably. What a predicament!

I sat on the edge of the bed and examined my foot. It had puffed up and turned a screaming-purple color. My God, what had I done last night?

I thought of John and knocked on the wall between our rooms. He came in quickly. "I can't walk. I must have hurt my foot more than I realized last night."

"Well, just stay in bed for now. After what you've been through, you deserve several days in bed."

"John, you don't understand. I need to get to the bathroom, now. Can you help me?"

"Oh, stupid me. Of course I'll just carry you across the hall. You're already sitting up so just let me slip my arms under your legs and off we go."

My T-shirt was rather short and somehow last night Mayme got my panties off along with my slacks. When John realized it was the bare me sitting on his arm he blushed deep burgundy. It embarrassed me, too, but it seemed more important to get to the lavatory than worry about modesty. He whisked me across the hall and then floundered around, not knowing what to do with me.

"Just put me on the toilet, please. This is no time to worry about the niceties. Now shut the door and come back in five minutes with my robe, if you can find it."

Before my next visit in here, we'd need to work out something a tad less embarrassing. John came right back and gave me a hand to stand. He slipped my robe around me and I tied the belt. After I stood on one foot to wash my hands he lifted me in his arms and we made it back to my room. What a relief to lie flat on the bed. I slid my foot out from under the covers and took another look at it. It had swelled to enormous proportions and resembled a large purple eggplant. What on earth did I do to it? Well, whatever the answer, I knew icing down my foot should be high on the list of important things to do.

John eyed my poor paw as if it were a poisonous snake. "Glennie, we have to do something about your foot. I think we better get you to a doctor. You need an X-ray and maybe you'll have to wear a cast. I'll get Mother up here to help you dress and then I'll make a few phone calls to find out where we should go."

"I hate all this fuss, but I think you're right about seeing a doctor. I've no idea how they handle foreigners in your medical system. I checked before I came over and added a travel rider to my insurance policy. Hope it covers me now that I'm working here. And, John, please give your mom a bag of ice for me."

Mayme arrived from the lower regions with the plastic sack of ice. "Please, Mrs. Fordyce, won't you help me get into some clothes. I don't think I can pull slacks or jeans on over my foot. See if you can find my brown tweed skirt in the closet. It's long and full and will keep me warm." She rummaged round and came back with the skirt and a half-slip to go under it. "In the second dresser drawer there's a gold sweater and right above it are some knee sox."

Mayme found the clothes I'd asked for. "I guess you can only wear one sock and shoe. It will hurt too much to tug a sock onto your sore foot."

John came back to report. "A Dr. McNab is in his surgery right now and if we hurry we can see him this morning. I have the truck out front with the engine running. Where's your coat?"

"I left it in cloakroom by the library and my purse should be with it. Oh, Mrs. Fordyce, would you hand me the hairbrush lying there on the dresser. I can't go out looking like an unmade bed." I smoothed down my hair and put on a dab of lipstick. "There, I guess I'll do."

John scooped me up in his arms and headed to the lift. Some wise soul put a chair in there and I could sit during the ride down. That made it easier on John. Poor man. I'm not fat at all, but I'm tall and my bones weigh heavy. He got me out the front door and into the truck and here came Jilly with a mug of tea for me.

"Bless you, Jilly. I need this desperately."

We drove for about ten minutes and then parked by a square concrete building. John rushed inside through the double doors and came right back out with a nurse pushing a wheelchair. I gulped the last of my tea and girded my loins, for I knew I was in for a bad time.

Inside the nurse pushed me right to an X-ray room. The technician took over. "Now, Miss James, if you'll just stand on that wee mat, I'll get a picture of your foot from the top. That looks to be where most of your damage is."

"I can't stand on it. I tried at home and almost passed out. Can't you do this some other way?"

She frowned at me as if I were a bad child. Well damn, it did hurt dreadfully.

"Let me see if I can have you sit on the edge of the table and aim the machine straight down. Yes, indeedy, that will work. Now turn over on your side. Doctor wants to see this foot from every angle."

By the time we got the ordeal over and I could sit back in the wheelchair, tears ran down my cheeks.

It upset John to see me hurting so much. He went to the receptionist. "Can't you give Miss James something for pain? She's miserable."

"I'm sorry, but Miss James will have to wait till the doctor examines her."

He seemed in no hurry to see me because an hour and twenty minutes passed before he came to my cubicle. He took a look at my foot and shot me a frown. After looking at the X-rays he turned back to me. "My God, girl, what on earth have you done? Does it hurt if

I press here, and how about here?"

I cringed. "You bet it hurts, it hurts everywhere."

"Well, tell me what happened."

"I got trapped into a sticky situation last night and I kicked a door trying to get free."

"How long did you kick the door? How many hours, that is? You couldn't have done this much damage with a few little kicks."

"My situation seemed pretty desperate and it took a long time before anyone heard me and came to my rescue."

This Dr. McNab was tall, thin, and sandy-haired. He gave me a sly grin. "I think there's more to the story than you've told me. Right?"

"Okay, Doc, I'll come clean." I pointed to John. "Mr. Fordyce and I manage the Hollystone House Bed-And-Breakfast north of the village. We had a difficult guest who drank too much last night and he trapped me in a room. I struggled with him and tried to make enough noise that someone would hear me. Fortunately someone did hear me banging the door and came to my rescue. I lay on my stomach on the floor with this person sitting on me, which is why I kicked with such desperation. So tell me the worst, Doctor."

Dr. McNab stepped back to the viewing light for another look at the X-rays. "Well, Miss James, you have multiple fractures of your foot. It's plainly smashed, rather like a bag of bone fragments." He pointed toward the X-rays with pencil, at what looked like small broken sticks. "You're going to have to take it very easy for a while."

John had been sitting quietly in a chair listening to the doctor. I motioned for him to step up near the exam table. "All right Doctor, give us the bad news."

"Well, you've smashed your foot all to hell and there are many small fractures through it, almost on top of each other. See in this picture, those lines are bone splinters sticking out in every direction. The treatment is going to be rest and time. For the next week the foot must be wrapped with an ace bandage. You can't bear any weight on it at all, miss, none. You may use a wheelchair and we'll give you crutches. They are only for places the wheelchair can't go."

Dr. McNab shook his head as he gave his orders. "Miss Bryson, check out a medium wheelchair and a pair of number eight crutches for Miss James. Now young lady, I'm dead serious about no weight on that foot. You should continue to keep ice on it and I'll write a prescription for pain. I want to see you back here in one week. We'll take another X-ray to see if healing has begun. If the swelling has diminished, we'll give you a boot cast, which you'll have to wear for five or six weeks. In about three weeks you can begin to bear weight on the foot and get more active with the crutches. Any questions?"

"I don't see how I can stay off my foot and do my work. What are we going to do, John?"

"Don't worry, Glennie. We'll manage. Thank you, Dr. McNab, for seeing her this morning. We appreciate your attention to Glenna."

"No problem. Say, what did you do with the fellow that caused this little incident?"

John and I looked at each other in shock. His face surged with color. "Oh my Lord. He's locked in a fourth floor bathroom. We forgot all about him this morning. We better get back because only Harry knows where he is and I expect he'll be afraid to let him out till I'm there. Ransome will either bang down the walls as Glennie did or be sleeping it off in a bathtub. Oh Gawd, we've got to hit the road." We were half laughing and half worried. I personally did not care how long Ransome stayed locked in that bathroom, but if he attracted the attention of the guests it could cause major upset.

We hurried back to the house. John carried me in and placed me in a chair by the fireplace. The entire Hollystone family gathered around me, full of questions. John made a second trip for the crutches and wheelchair and then he took over the explanations. "Glennie's foot is smashed and she's not to bear one ounce of weight on it. She'll use the wheelchair to get around the house. The crutches are to be used only in tight spots where the wheelchair won't fit. She's got to keep her foot elevated and have an ice pack several times a day. And she must rest."

Everyone began to talk at once. Mayme's voice spoke louder than the others. "I'll take over your work, Glenna."

Jilly leaned down to whisper to me. "I don't have to take any time off for the next few weeks. Then you won't have to fill in for me at breakfast and tea time, Glennie."

I interrupted them. "John and I'll work things out. We may have to call on all of you for extra help, but with a little rearranging of schedules we'll get the work done. There'll be many things I can handle sitting down, like answering the phone, ordering supplies, and taking reservations. Give us today to get organized. But what about Ransome? Have you found him yet?"

They all looked blank and John ran for the elevator. He came back down holding Ransome in an arm lock. He shoved him into a chair near me. Lady Sheila glared at him and he shrank down like a little kid.

"Son, I'm mortally ashamed of you. This is the last straw. You are to leave this house within the hour. Don't come back till you're self-supporting. I'll call Guy today and tell him to cancel your allowance. You get out of here and find a job. I am deadly serious. I don't want to see you again until you've found work and can take care of yourself. Goodbye, son."

She held a hankie to her eyes to stem the tears but she didn't back down.

Ransome knelt down by her chair. "Mother, don't do this to me. I can't get a job. I don't know how to do anything. Who would hire me?" All eyes were on them. The scene had us so hypnotized we were unable to look away.

"I don't know who would hire you but I expect you can dig ditches. You've had every opportunity to help out here but you've avoided any job you've been asked to do. All your life you've let others do the work for you but that will stop. Now collect your things and be gone." She sat down abruptly. Her hands shook and her face looked pale. Mayme stepped over and felt her pulse. She saw me watching her and nodded that it was okay.

John volunteered, "I'll drive him to the bus stop."

"No, you won't, John. He can walk wherever he's going." Our Lady hung tough but I knew it cost her dearly.

"What if I apologize to Glenna and promise never to do anything like this again?"

"It's too late, Ransome. Get on your way now." Lady Sheila began openly sobbing, but she stood her ground. Ransome's life of ease was over.

The scene left us all rather shaken and it took time to get back to the reorganization of our work schedule. Jilly woke up to the fact that I hadn't eaten and she dashed to the kitchen for tea. When she returned with a tray I pointed out that John had missed breakfast also, so she came up with an extra cup and we shared the cranberry muffins.

After I settled on a sofa in the library, John made a trip to the pharmacy in the village to get my pain medication. I reached for two of the white pills when he returned. All this tearing around in the truck and in and out of the doctor's office left me with a throbbing in my foot that wouldn't quit.

While we waited for the pills to work, John sat by me and I reached for his hand. "I think your mother can be a big help to us. She's offered and if you have no objections, let's ask her to do the running I usually do. She can get the mail and bring it to me to sort. She can check supplies and tell me what to order. I've thought lately of asking her to be in charge of the housemaids. She wouldn't need to do any of the work, just check the rooms. Let's ask her to take on that chore. She seems young enough and is full of energy. I think she'd like some responsibilities."

"Excellent idea, Glennie. How about you taking the rest of today off? I'll get you an afghan and settled you on the library sofa. Why don't we just make this your daytime hideaway? We can put your computer on the desk. The phone's handy and you can do what you feel up to and rest in between."

"Sounds like a plan to me. What I really need is a maid, someone to bring me ice and help me to the loo. I'm afraid I'll be an awful nuisance with my wants and needs."

"I'll be your wee maid — no, I think I'd rather be your footman. I'm always running around the building. I'll pop in regularly and see what you need." He rummaged in the desk and found a pad and pen. He laid these on the table beside the sofa. He moved the phone where I could reach it. "I'm off for a coverlet and an ice bag."

I called after him as he reached the door. "There's a book in my room that I'd like to have, please. And could you bring the pillows off my bed and a towel to wrap up the ice bag?"

John grinned at me and saluted. "Anything else, your majesty?"
"No, slave, that will be all for now."

When he returned from the bar with the ice and came down from the fourth floor with the other things I felt drowsy from the pills. He helped me into the wheelchair and pushed me to the loo. I stood on one foot and sat after he went out. When he returned, he pulled me up on my foot and whisked me into the chair. Back on the sofa, he arranged my bed pillows, placed the ice in a towel around my foot, and covered me with a quilt. He laid my book within reach on the table and lastly he bent down and gave me a sweet kiss on the lips.

"Rest well, Glennie." With that, he left, closing the door quietly.

CHAPTER 24

The next day the household ran smoothly. John's mother took over the supervision of the maids, and she seemed to enjoy bringing them up to her standards. A rumor traveled around the house that she wore white gloves to check on the dusting. Mayme personally sorted the sheets before the maids laundered them. She also kept a close count of the small shampoo bottles to make sure they weren't smuggled home in a maid's pocket. I doubted she acted so tough that the women would quit and she seemed to thrive in her job.

When a week had passed, John drove me to see Dr. McNab again. After another X-ray, the doctor came in to tell us the results. "Well, missy, you must be behaving yourself. I see signs of healing and you can move into a Velcro cast. Take it off to shower but you must have help. A fall at this stage would be disastrous. Otherwise, keep it on all the time."

When the doctor finished the exam, he grinned at me. "Well, any more drunken guests tried to assault you lately?"

I smiled back at him. "When they do, I hit them with my crutch. Which reminds me, can I use them more now?"

"Yes, but go easy, just try them a bit each day. If anything hurts, back off. I want to see you again in three weeks."

Immediately the cast gave better support to my leg. That helped diminish the pain so I could cut back on the pain pills.

Lady Sheila continued to handle the check-in and every morning she paid me a fifteen-minute visit to talk about how things were going around the house. She seemed so cheerful that I always felt a lift from her chats. One morning she spoke hesitantly. "My dear, I hate to bring this up, but I feel I must apologize for what Ransome did to you. If only we'd been more firm with him earlier, this might not have happened."

"Ma'am, don't feel this was your fault. Some people are just born troublemakers and I doubt there's a thing you could've done to change him. Besides, I'm the one who hurt myself. He only taped my mouth shut and sat on me. I kicked the door and did the damage. Be thankful for Guy. Tell me what you hear from him."

"I called him in Saudi Arabia right after you were hurt. He sent you best wishes for your recovery and said he'd try to get home soon. He also agreed not to give Ransome any more money."

I nodded my agreement. "That's probably the best thing you could do. Now don't think about Ransome or feel responsible. I'm doing fine."

In the afternoons after Jamie's nap, Ellen would bring the boy to see me for a few minutes. He had grown into a round-cheeked chunk of a baby. His nanny would put a quilt on the floor and lay him on his tummy. He could roll over now and Ellen beamed with pride at his accomplishments. She'd chatter on about his virtues and then whisk him away to have playtime with his mother before Jilly went down to prepare the guests' tea.

After a couple of weeks I spent some of each day at the desk. I could deal with the written reservations and the phone. I entered all data into the computer and printed out a daily roster of arriving guests. Jilly would bring her food orders to me in the mornings along with a tea tray and whatever breakfast goodies the guests didn't eat. We talked things over and discussed occasional menu changes.

After dinner in the evening I could wheel my chair to the elevator and go to my room. Every night Mayme would help me take a shower and then rewrap my ace bandage or later put my cast back on. Things moved along quite well and I hoped no one became seriously overworked because of my injury. The wheelchair would roll right up to the table in the morning room for meals, as well as to my desk to work. I could dress myself and make it to the bathroom alone and it boosted my spirits to be independent again.

John treated me so sweetly after my injury. He ran my errands, brought me treats, and kept the ice bag filled. To celebrate my new level of freedom, one day he took me to lunch in the pub. It felt grand to be out in the world. Much as I enjoyed working in the library, a bad case of cabin fever had moved in with me.

He helped me out of the truck and I crutched my way into the Crown & Anchor. "How about fish and chips, Glennie?"

"Bring them on. I'm ready for a large greasy lunch."

I took a big bite of fish that I'd sprinkled with vinegar. "When I go upstairs this evening, I'm going to wheel down the hall and check out the new construction. I want to see what Harry and the Jardines have accomplished with the remodeling and then plan the decor. I've thought of paisleys for spreads and window treatments. I have a sample of a tartan carpet that would be great on the floor."

"What's a window treatment?"

"It's curtains or draperies, except they cost more. Surely you've learned that much from all of our decorating."

John laughed and we had a fun lunch. It seemed to me the time I spent with John satisfied something in me. When I worked or rested in the library, I constantly listened for his footsteps to come down the hall. I felt as if he never stayed long enough and I found myself searching for reasons to keep him there with me. Something had happened to my feelings but the thought of exploring them scared me. I'd tell myself that I'd think about how I felt later. So foolish of me.

When Guy arrived to visit us, he came due to a summons from John because Lady Sheila came down with pneumonia. First she caught a cold. The cough hung on and turned into bronchitis, which moved down into her lungs. Mayme came into the library one morning. "Glennie, I think Sheila's getting worse. She's running a fever. Would you call the clinic and see what they think we should do?"

The receptionist said Dr. McNab would stop in on his lunch hour to see her. That impressed me. I couldn't imagine that a doctor from the National Health Service would make a house call. Maybe it helped to have Lady in front of one's name.

I could use the crutches easily now. When Dr. McNab walked in the front door, he caught me moving from the library to the check-in desk. "Afternoon, Miss James. How's that foot? Are you avoiding out of control guests?"

"Things have been calm recently, Doctor. We're just worried about Lady Sheila. Here's Mr. Fordyce. He'll take you to her room." The doctor nodded and followed John through the hall.

Later John called Guy from the library and I overheard the conversation. "She's not dangerously ill, but the doctor says rest and antibiotics are a must. You might want to come and see how she is for yourself."

Guy agreed that he needed to see his mother and blew into Hollystone House the next day. I heard him come in the front door and went out to meet him. "Glennie, how well you handle those crutches. It's wonderful to see you up and about. I feared I'd find both you and mother flat on your backs. How is Mother?"

"She's improving slowly. Right now she sleeps quite a bit. She'll be pleased to see you."

"Is someone with her?"

"John's mother is quite attentive. She sits and reads to Lady Sheila most afternoons. Go on to her room and see how she is for yourself."

A couple of days after Guy's arrival, he found me typing away at the computer. "Glenna, how is your foot healing?"

"It's going back together quite well. The doctor seems to think it'll mend completely."

"I feel dreadful that my nasty brother attacked you. Mother is terribly upset about his behavior. What can we do to make amends?"

"I don't blame either one of you. I did the damage to myself when I kicked the door so hard."

He shook his head at me. "Ransome is at fault, no question. Will your stateside insurance pay for your treatment?"

I shifted in my wheelchair. "Actually, it doesn't. Illness yes, accident no. I should have read the fine print."

"Then I'll take care of it. Not only are you my employee but if not for my rascally brother you wouldn't be hurt."

I started to speak but he held up his hand. "Not another word. I'll tell John to pay the bill."

"Thanks you, Guy. I appreciate your concern."

"Glenna, tell me how things are going for you? Do you expect to make a career of managing inns or do you have plans to return to Chicago and your business?"

I pushed my wheelchair back from the desk. "I haven't thought that much about the future, Guy. I'm happy doing what I'm involved in right now. If things change here I probably could get a job at any large hotel. I love decorating and I suppose working my way back into the business is possible. Certainly the work I've done for you would look good on my résumé."

"How about marriage? Does that figure in your future plans?"

He surprised me but I managed to answer coolly enough. "Certainly I hope to marry one day. I want children as much or more as I want a career. Guess I'm waiting for opportunity to knock."

"Hmm. He paused as if to make a decision. "I admire you a great deal, Glenna. You seem to know what you want out of life while I whiz around the globe chasing moonbeams or fireflies. Have you thought about moving to England permanently?"

"Yes, I've considered it. Where I live isn't nearly as important as whom I live with. If the right person came along, I could live in an igloo in Alaska. And you know, with parents like mine, going home again holds no charm. The next time I show up in the U.S., I better have a husband in tow."

Guy laughed, leaned close, and put his hand on mine. "Right, I understand. Well, my dear, I want to know if you've considered me as husband material?"

"Guy, I don't know you that well. How could I tell what kind of a husband you'd be? Right now you're like a comet streaking across the sky. That old saw, 'Absence makes the heart grow fonder,' is nonsense. In my book closeness is what makes love grow."

"What if I stayed here for the next month? Do you think you could become fond of me in that amount of time?"

"Wow! You're full of surprises. Wouldn't you go nuts with nothing to do?"

"Oh, I'd have plenty to do. Some of my business dealings are manageable from here. All I need is a fax machine and the Internet. Besides, I'd like to help run this place. It's mine and I don't know anything about it or how it works. Wouldn't there be something I could do here at the inn?" He looked at me with such a pleading expression.

"How's your back? One of the big jobs is humping the luggage to the rooms and back down again. Harry is busy painting up on fourth and he could really use some help with his other chores. Jilly's kitchen helper left to go to cooking school two weeks ago." Guy began to frown but I went relentlessly on. "Perhaps you could learn to load the dishwasher and bring up the tea tray. Your Aunt Mayme would find an extra maid very useful on weekends. Could you make square corners on the beds? Just jump in here if any of these jobs fit your curriculum vitae."

He pulled his chair up closer to the desk. "If nothing else I could hang around and laugh at the funny things you say. But I do have an idea. John hasn't had a holiday for several years. Maybe he'd like to take a trip and I could fill in for him. It isn't beyond my skills to make out bills for the guests and check them out of a morning. I'm sure I could pour drinks for our guests. And with the elevator and a hand trolley, I could shift luggage with the best of bellhops."

"Say that's a great idea. I'm going to order one of those luggage carts right away. It would really take the pressure off if we had an easy way to move the bags. Oh, another thing, you'd have to do an early morning run to the village bakeshop on the days Jilly doesn't make scones. I can't function mornings until I have them with my tea. Sometimes I crave them in the afternoons too and that has become one of John's chores." I heard myself rattling on foolishly and decided to become more serious. "Also in a few weeks someone has to drive me to see Dr. McNab again. John and I see our functions here like that old Chicago jazz expression, 'we double in brass.'"

"Meaning you fill in where needed. I've heard some jazz in the windy city. All right, how would you fit me into the overall scheme of things if I decide to stay for a time?"

"First, you must talk to John. After all, if you're sending him on holiday he should have time to decide where he's going. He might want to pack a bag before you shove him out the door." I felt panic at the thought of John leaving. It didn't seem as if Guy could take his place.

Guy sailed out of the library and left me to rerun all the things he'd said back through my head. His approach as a lover seemed awkward in the extreme. When I first met Guy, the idea of marrying him seemed quite attractive. Since he'd only made rather clumsy efforts to pursue me, I'd about crossed him off my list. Right now I wasn't sure who or what I wanted for a mate, but if I were smart I'd think about it soon.

I'd returned to the computer when Guy hurried back into the library and John, looking angry, followed in his wake. "What are you two plotting behind my back?"

"Hey, it's your cousin, not me." I looked at John, hoping he'd glance my way. I wanted to shake my head no but he kept his eyes on Guy.

I sat quietly and let Guy muddle through an explanation. "John, Glenna and I think you're overworked. I know you haven't been on holiday for at least three years. We really believe you should take some time off before you have a nervous collapse. You could go to Brighton or maybe try sailing out of Poole. How about a walking tour of Wales? Or Cornwall, yes Cornwall. We have that old cousin of Dad's who lives near Bodmin Moor. What do you think about a visit to him?"

"I think you're bloody crazy is what I think. Glennie, tell me what's happening."

"Your cousin Guy is talking about becoming domesticated and would like to try staying here for a month. I don't see it working very well, but he wants to take over your share of the chores. You probably do need a vacation after you've worked so long for this slave driver. Now you two iron out the details and let me get on with my work. Please let me know what you decide, but in the meantime don't bother me any longer with your nonsense."

I could hear John slam around the library and bang his way through the Great Hall. As a grown man, taking vacations should be his idea, not someone else's. Well, maybe with him away I could come to some conclusions about my feelings for these two men.

They left in the Land Rover and I heard no more out of them until after lunch, which they missed entirely. They went to the pub and smelled decidedly beery when they sidled into the library. I lay on the sofa for a brief rest so they spouted apologies for disturbing me. I sat up and glared at them. "Okay, just tell me who's going away and when. You know we're trying to run a business here while you clowns are creating havoc."

CHAPTER 25

What a weird three weeks. Not only because I missed John enormously, but also because our resident ghost, Minerva Padget, paid us a visit. She began in a small way, startling us with an occasional groan. The guests would mention hearing strange sounds at night.

Lady Sheila had recovered from her illness and when we discussed the ghost, she blamed the noises on the wind. She mentioned that parts of the house were centuries old. When Minerva began dragging chains down the steps at night, it alarmed some of us. Guy was no help and he loved to regale the guests with stories about Minerva's past. I caught him at it in the bar one evening.

"Yes, it's true. Poor Lady Minerva was desperate. She died birthing her thirteenth child and became so bitter at Lord Donovan for getting her with child at her time of life that she just wouldn't go to her grave quietly."

I wanted to laugh, yet his careless attitude made me angry. Yes, the guests gathered around to hear him tell his tales, but we couldn't afford to have our clientele scared away. He declared it was good for business, but I wondered.

John called nearly every day. The connections were often bad and the calls seemed unsatisfactory. I would answer the phone and hear this faint voice. "How's it going, Glennie?"

I'd shout back at him. "Fine. We're all fine. Where are you?"

It took three calls before I understood that he went to Scotland instead of Cornwall. I hollered into the phone, "What are you doing up there?"

"Looking into something — something," he'd shout back. His calls left me upset and I found myself staring into space when I should be ordering food supplies.

Guy manfully shouldered John's tasks. He wasn't too bad at preparing the bills and checking people out, but every morning I had to remind him to include the bar tabs. What he did best was act as "mine host." He dispensed drinks at the bar while he told ribald stories. He flirted with the women guests and slapped the men on the back. Boy, did I miss John. Guy did the chores and errands we asked him to handle. He simply couldn't replace John.

One call from John came in on a clear line and we were finally able to talk. I reported on the ghost and complained about Guy's shortcomings. John laughed. "I wouldn't put it past Guy to have activated the ghost himself. Have you checked the attic for chains or anything suspicious?"

"No, I'm still not able to get up those stairs, but my cast comes off next week and then I'll go look."

He was immediately concerned. "Be careful you don't fall on the narrow steps. I'll be home in a week and I can check then."

"What are you doing up there? Are you walking or seeing people?"

"I'm not doing either one. I'm handling some estate work for Lady Sheila and also for Mum. There were several family concerns that I needed to deal with and I'll have things in good shape soon."

"Doesn't seem like much of a vacation to me."

"It isn't a holiday. Most of the work I'm doing is for Guy and Lady Sheila. I may want some time off later when it's warmer. These are things I had to do sometime and it's a relief to get them cleared up. I'll tell you all about it when I come home." Home, he thought of Hollystone House as home.

Guy didn't waste time acting like a suiter suitor during this time. He stopped into the library or at my desk a dozen times a day to visit with me. Some evenings after his bar tending duties were over he'd take me out for a late dinner. We went to the pub a couple of times and once to a supper club. That wasn't much fun as people were dancing and I hated that I had to stay off my foot.

We had some lively conversations, but the good night kisses seemed to be fading in intensity. They didn't stir my blood like the ones I remembered from Las Vegas. It worried me. Guy went through the motions of courting me and I knew we were working toward a conclusion of some sort.

When John called, I felt his anger come through the phone line. I hoped it was Guy being there that upset him. I felt fairly sure he knew Guy had shoved him out of the way to have my attention full-time. Well, he must be right. Guy acted as if he was headed toward a proposal. I wasn't at all sure I wanted to hear it.

A final visit to the doctor required one more X-ray. He pronounced me healed and I joyfully left the boot cast and crutches behind in his office. I said goodbye to the wheelchair with great pleasure. Guy took me to lunch to celebrate my recovery. He foolishly ordered champagne and I wisely only drank one glass. He had several so I drove the truck home. It was a tough trip as I'd seldom driven since coming to England. My foot didn't work well for using the clutch but I managed.

I drove up the long drive and parked behind a handsome green Jaguar Saloon. Guy seemed as puzzled by it as I was, since it was early for guests to arrive. We hurried in to see who drove such a new and stylish car.

John sat by the fireplace. When we came in the front door, he jumped up and almost ran to us. He threw his arms around me and gave me a magnificent hug. It thrilled me and my knees started to tremble. I wanted to kiss him, but Guy's presence made me hold back. Jilly summoned Guy to the phone immediately so he went to the library. I sat down by the fire to talk to be near John.

"Where did you get that magnificent mustache?"

"Well, I went into a store in Edinburgh and when I saw it, I had to have it."

"Silly, I love it. Would it tickle, do you think?"

John brushed his lips and the mustache across my cheek and it did, tickle that is. I giggled.

"Whose wonderful car is that out front?"

"Mine. I'm tired of driving that ratty old Land Rover so I bought a car in Scotland and drove back overnight. How are you, Glennie? You look wonderful."

"I have my cast off, see. I must take a bit of care of my foot yet but it's mended beautifully. Now tell me what you were doing so long in Scotland. Did you look up any of your old girlfriends?"

"Oh, yeah. There were dozens of them lined up to see me. Actually I sold my parents' home, the place where I grew up. Mother doesn't want to live in the country any more. We agreed that if she leaves here, she could get a nice flat in the city. She wouldn't mind being near the theatres and shopping that London has to offer. I also arranged for repairs to Lady Sheila's crumbling castle. I think she should sell it too, but she's not quite ready to let it go."

"You were a busy boy. Doing all that and buying a car too. I've forgotten what it's like to ride in a classy automobile."

He grinned like a little boy. "Come for a spin right now. You still have your coat on. Let's go."

He led me through the front door in a rush as Guy came out of the library. He yelled after us but we were heedless and quickly John had us speeding down the drive to the main highway. What a heady feeling to be on the road like this in a fast car. It felt as if we were flying.

On the main thoroughfare John braked to a stop in a little lay-by and pulled me roughly against him. He gave me the kiss I'd wanted when I first saw him there by the fire. Let me report that the electricity flowed between us and there were no thoughts of fabric samples darting through my mind. One kiss followed another and in a short time we both were breathless. And oh, I loved that mustache.

"Glennie, you don't know how I missed you. I literally ached for you. Please tell me you yearned for me to come home."

I didn't know quite where we were headed but I had to answer him honestly. "I did. I've just spent the longest three weeks of my life. Every day there were things I wanted to share with you, things to talk about. You can't possibly know how glad I am to see you. I didn't want you to go away, but I didn't know how to say it as Guy rushed you out the door."

"I think it's time for us to get things out in the open. Did Guy pay you a lot of attention while I was away?"

"He tried. We chatted in the library; we went to the pub for dinner. We were together, but it wasn't the same. I couldn't get excited about him. I just put in time until you came back."

An edge came into John's voice. "I boiled with anger as I rode the train to Scotland. I didn't want to go away and leave you to Guy. I figured I'd come back and find you engaged to him and the thought made me furious. I made up my mind that if you'd made a commitment to Guy, I'd do everything in my power to break it up. You haven't made any promises to him, have you?"

"Not one. All the attention Guy paid me only made me realize that he wasn't the person for me. There was no emotion, no feeling that I couldn't live without him."

"And what man did you think you couldn't live without?"

I looked at him and answered very softly. "It was you." He tightened his hold on me and the strength of his arms made me feel so cherished, so loved.

"Glenna James, I adore you. Will you marry me?"

An electric thrill shot clear through me as I nodded my head. It took a minute before I could speak. "Oh John, I will marry you. I'm ready whenever you say."

He began to dig around in his coat pocket. Then he stopped and pulled me so close that my breath caught. The kiss he gave me blotted out everything else. It was just John's lips pressed against mine. All I could think was, yes, this is what I want. Please let him kiss me forever.

When we had to stop and breathe, John continued to search his pockets for something. "Ah-hah, I knew it was here somewhere." He produced a small box, opened the hinged lid, and showed me a diamond solitaire ring. The stone, cut in a marquise shape, glittered like the sun. He slipped it on my finger. "Glennie, I love you with all my heart."

I turned into a pile of mush. Tears flooded out of my eyes and even John's eyes glistened with moisture. What a beautiful moment. The best of my life.

Then we settled down and I opened my heart to John. "First of all, I love you so much. I've struggled with it for months now. I came here feeling somewhat committed to Guy, but your face kept getting in the way. I kept putting off dealing with my feelings. I would think about you and Guy and then back off. I figured there was always tomorrow to decide what I wanted."

"Oh, Glennie dear, you're a treasure. I want to shout our engagement to the world, but in the meantime should we go into the house beaming like idiots and make our big announcement or shall we keep it mum for a time?"

"I'd like to wait a little bit. I think I owe it to Guy to tell him privately. Let's see how that goes before we trumpet the news. However, I'm going to wear my ring no matter what. If someone notices it, so be it. Please give me another one of those kisses. I don't think I'll ever get enough of them." I reached for his lips and felt a fire start in my chest.

CHAPTER 26

The entire Hollystone gang sat around the fireplace when we got back. The women felt some vibrations about our sudden escape and the men wanted to see the new car. I kept my left hand in my pocket and smiled blandly while John took Guy, Harry, and the Jardines out to see his automobile.

When they trooped into the house, I crooked a finger at Guy and led him to the library. I shut the door in a couple of nosy faces so we could be alone.

"Guy, I need to tell you something. You may have guessed that I told John I'd marry him."

His face flushed a dark red. "Marry! Marry John! How did this happen? I've tried to change myself into the person you wanted and here you go behind my back and decide to marry my cousin. God, Glenna, did I wait too long? I thought I needed to go slow and woo you gently. What did I do wrong?"

"John had something to offer that you didn't, Guy. He stayed here with me all the time. We worked together and we laughed together. We've been a team as we slaved away on your house. He's a wonderful, sweet man, and I fell for him like a ton of bricks."

"Well, I feel like a fool. I planned to propose to you. What do you think of that?"

"I'm glad you waited. Do you think you love me?"

"Well, I like you a whole lot."

I frowned at him. "Like isn't in the ball game, fella. If it isn't love, it won't fly. John and I love each other. It's been growing for months while we moved furniture and hung curtains. It developed over early

148

morning scones and tea. It slipped in during visits to the clinic with a broken foot. You weren't here and he was."

Guy began to pace the narrow confines of the library. "But, I took you to the doctor just today. And I was here with you all the time John was away. Doesn't that count?"

"Three weeks doesn't make a love affair. I could never marry you, Guy. The chemistry isn't there."

He took a deep breath and when he let it out he looked as deflated as a child's balloon. "Well, Glenna, I'm sorry to lose you but it couldn't be to a better man." He gave me a kiss on the cheek and went to the door. Then he turned back to me. "I'll be leaving in the morning. I need to pack. Thank goodness Mother recovered from her illness."

So much for the thwarted lover. He didn't seem to be bleeding from a broken heart. I felt only relief that our strange affair had ended without fireworks.

Time seemed to telescope and I realized Jilly had served tea to the guests in the hall. I'd go out later and encourage them to play card games. Or perhaps turn on the telly so the men could watch the news.

Jilly came back up from the kitchen and set the big tray in the morning room for the Hollystone family. Ellen came in with Jamie. He'd become so active she could barely hang on to him. He scooted all around his playpen and would soon pull himself up on his feet. I felt envy when I looked at his beautiful little face. I hoped John and I could have babies like Jamie.

I kept my ring hand in my lap and enjoyed a hearty tea. Jilly's liver pate sandwiches and frosted cookies tasted especially good.

When Jilly and I cleared the table Mayme noticed my ring. "Glennie, you have a diamond. When did you get it? Have you had it long? Let me see it. Who gave it to you?"

Mayme was no fool and surely her eye had been on John and me for some time. I held the ring out for the others to admire. It looked pretty impressive, being all of two carats. Ellen and Lady Sheila oohed and aahed over it and I winked at John above their heads.

Again the question came. "Who gave you the ring? You must tell us the name of the lucky fellow." The Jardine maids craned their necks to look first at Guy and then at John.

John sat quietly in a corner of the morning room with a small smile on his face. I decided to play to the crowd with a little drama. I stood up and looked around the room. Then I walked over, sat on John's lap, and gave him a big kiss. "John's the one."

It made for a dramatic moment and I enjoyed it to the max. It may have been cruel to Guy, but I felt with his rare visits and his lack of attention to me he didn't deserve much consideration. He responded as the gentleman he is, shook John's hand, and gave me a chaste kiss on the cheek.

Mayme grabbed me in an enormous hug. "Welcome to the Fordyce family, Glennie. I'm terribly pleased about this. Have you made any plans for the wedding or where you'll live?"

John frowned at her. "Mother, give us some time. We've only been engaged about an hour."

I could see my role of family peacemaker develop already. "As soon as we get organized, we'll let you know, Mrs. Fordyce."

She immediately came to hug me again. "Please call me Mayme. There's no reason to be so formal with us soon to be family."

Lady Sheila, always gracious, held me in a sweet hug and whispered in my ear. "I'd hoped to be your mother-in-law, my dear, but I think a great deal of John and know he'll make you happy."

Jilly gave me a quick squeeze. "We're so happy for you, Miss Glennie." Dear old inarticulate Harry patted me on the shoulder and grinned. He also shook John's hand.

With only Ellen left I waited for her to comment in her dour voice. "Best wishes, I'm sure, miss and Mr. John." I know she imagined we'd leaped in and out of each other's beds for months.

John and I wanted to spend the evening together and talk about so many things. We couldn't seem to get away from the family and I needed to pay a little attention to our guests. I got his attention and pulled him aside. "I'll meet you upstairs at nine. That will be our time."

"Right, wild horses won't keep me away." What made the idea of meeting upstairs exciting was the realization that sometime, before long, we would make love for the first time. If not tonight, it would be soon. The anticipation had me on a high.

A bit later Jilly came to me with some strange news. "Miss Glennie, I keep finding bits of food missing. If I lay out muffins for breakfast a few of them will be gone in the morning. It's never a whole lot, but someone has helped themselves to a loaf of bread here and a cube of butter there. I can't imagine who's doing it. The daily maids are long gone by the time I get food out of the freezer. Who in this household doesn't get enough to eat at mealtimes?"

"It's a puzzle. Do you think some of the guests are making midnight raids?"

She shook her head. "That's hard to believe because it happens almost every day. The guests change nearly every day and surely we wouldn't have a food thief staying here each night."

"Let me think about it, Jilly. Maybe we could set some kind of trap and catch whoever's doing the dirty deed. Was it happening before Guy came and John left?"

"It started about the time Mr. John left."

I stood up and headed toward the door. "I simply can't believe Guy would steal food from his own kitchen. He's leaving in the morning and I'll just straight out ask him before he goes. In fact, he's in the library and I'll speak to him now."

I quickly worked up a head of steam and headed for the library. I burst in without knocking. "Guy, are you making midnight raids on the kitchen? Someone is and Jilly is rather concerned."

"Good God no! Jilly feeds us enough that there's no need to have more. Could it be Ellen? Sometimes old people get crazy ideas about not having enough food and will collect a secret supply. What a situation."

"I know. I wish we could lay some kind of snare and trap the culprit. I'll give it some thought tonight and maybe have an idea in the morning. Good night, Guy."

I rode up in the elevator, to baby my foot a bit longer. When it grew stronger, I'd use the steps as good exercise and rehab therapy. I tapped on John's door and he opened it immediately, pulled me into his room, and sat down in a big easy chair with me on his lap. He pulled me close for some of his magical kisses. They made me feel like dancing on the ceiling. Then we talked about the foolish things that lovers do. How wonderful to be alone and not feel as if our romance took place in front of the entire family. Impulsively I walked to the door and turned the lock.

"Let's keep things as private as possible, shall we?"

"Definitely. I think we're going to have trouble with Mum. She'll be forever after us—ask, ask, asking the questions. You know, Glennie, we have some big decisions to make. Are we going to stay here and run this inn with our extended family? Or do we want to pull clear away? I can do most of Guy's bookkeeping almost anywhere with a computer and fax machine. We could go back to Chicago and live in your house. Would you like that?"

"No, I wouldn't. My mother would call us every month to see if I was pregnant. Which reminds me." I leaned back to look directly at him. "How do you feel about children? Do you want some?"

"Yes, some. Shall we put in an order for two or three? You know, if we stay in England, my mum will check every month to see if your condition is delicate."

"I think I can handle her better than my own mother. Speaking of which or whom, I suppose I better tell them the good news and try to patch up things. Good grief, we have to decide where we'll get married. I truly don't know whether I can stand a full-blown wedding with eight bridesmaids and the whole shot. My brother, Michael, always referred to his and Sarah's extravaganza as the dog and pony show. I would really prefer a nice wedding like Jilly and Harry's. It seemed perfect."

"That sounds good to me. I feel as if we're a little long in the tooth for the big showy nuptials."

I laughed at him then. "Which reminds me, how old are you anyhow?"

"Two weeks ago, while I was in Scotland, I reached the advanced age of thirty-five."

"John, you celebrated your birthday all alone! How awful. I'll have to make it up to you."

"Right now all I want for my birthday is you, you in the flesh, and in my bed. Think you could arrange that?"

"Yes, I've wondered when we'd get to that. On one hand I can't wait, but then when I think about holding off a bit to savor the experience that also has appeal. What do you think?"

"I think you're a bit of a tease and tonight isn't soon enough. Don't be cruel, Glennie."

At this crucial point Minerva Padget came awake. She let us know of her presence and that she wasn't happy. The moans seemed to come from John's closet. We rushed to the door and found nothing, but then John began to tap on the walls. There were hollow sounds on one side. "I think there's a long shaft just outside the west wall of the closet. For some reason they did things like that when they built these old houses. It might have been a dumbwaiter or a place to chuck the dirty linen down to the laundry."

The moans came again and I felt the hair on the back of my neck stand up.

John unlocked the door and stepped into the hall. "I think the moans may be coming from the attics. Let's go look." As I came up beside him, he put a finger to his lips and eased the attic door open.

He started up the stairs, which were steep, and I trailed right behind him. As we got to the top and hesitated about whether to turn right or left, a man burst from the right side of the first attic. He got by John, but in his fury to escape he ran smack into me, and down the steps we went, ass over teakettle, to land in a heap on the floor outside John's bedroom.

And there I lay entangled with my old buddy Ransome. John flew down the stairs and narrowly avoided stepping on our prone bodies. Ransome had the wind knocked out of him so John corralled him and hauled him off me. Then he simply swung Ransome around and down the hall to the same bathroom he'd been locked in before. John is so strong and muscular that he made handling Ransome look easy.

I knew at once the fall had re-injured my foot and I concentrated on trying not to yell or faint from the pain.

I must have hollered something because Jilly and Harry rushed out of their apartment and bent over me. Guy stepped off the elevator, followed by Mayme. John came back, scooped me up in his arms, turned into his room, and laid me on the bed. Everyone asked questions at once so John just waited till they quieted down one by one.

"Our ghost is Ransome. He sneaked into the house and camped out in the attics. At the moment he's back locked in the hall bathroom again. I wonder what he's been eating?"

A look of astonishment spread over Jilly's face. "Oh, my gosh! He took the food."

I struggled to sit up but the pain in my foot forced me to lie back down. "Or course, Ransome's our thief."

Jilly told the others about missing food from the kitchen. "He'd wait till we went to bed and then slip down to the ground floor and raid the pantry for supplies."

Everyone began talking at once and Mayme moved to the bedside. "Glenna, are you hurt? You look very uncomfortable lying there on John's bed." Did I hear a note of disapproval in her voice? Thank heavens, both John and I were fully dressed. I'm not sure what state we'd have been in if the ghost had surfaced later in the evening.

Jilly spoke up quickly. "Harry and I saw it happen. Miss Glenna climbed up the stairs to the attic and Mr. Ransome simply ran her down as he tried to get away. I expect she's hurt her foot again."

I frowned and nodded my head. "Right. I think I'm bruised from stem to stern. My foot got several good whacks as we fell. I didn't have time to count how many times Ransome and I somersaulted as we came down the steps. I landed under him and right now everything hurts."

John slipped off my shoe and sock. "I'm going to see if I can take Glennie to see Dr. McNab. She should be checked over and perhaps have X-rays again. I'll go down and call him."

While he was gone, I wanted some answers. "Did all of you hear the ghost moaning tonight or did you come up because Ransome and I landed with a crash?"

Jilly slipped an extra pillow under my foot. "We heard the moans and saw the crash. We were actually out in the hall when you landed. I hope you've not broken your back, Miss Glennie. You lit awful hard."

Mayme seemed a bit more relaxed than at first. "I heard the moans. My room is right under John's, and I think there's a channel in the wall where he directed the sound. You poor girl, Ransome got you again. That boy is demented. I truly hate to have to tell his mother he caused all this fuss. She'll be devastated."

I couldn't bear to see Lady Sheila upset by this. "Could we forget to tell Lady Sheila? I think if she believes he's gone off somewhere and maybe gotten a job, she'll feel much better than if we make her face up to his latest fiasco. What do you say?" I stared up at the faces above me. "If she doesn't ask about the commotion, we won't tell her anything. Or we can say the wind caused the moaning. Agreed?"

Guy, the first to speak, went along with my suggestion and everyone else hastily agreed to the deception. "We'll just tell her that you tripped, Glennie."

CHAPTER 27

John came up in the elevator to report. "Dr. McNab just delivered a baby at the Cottage Hospital and he's about to head home. He agreed to stop here in about ten minutes and look over your injuries."

Guy headed toward the steps. "I'll meet the doctor at the door and bring him up."

Mayme took charge and began to give orders. "We better get you into your room, Glenna, so you can be undressed and ready for the doctor's exam. John, you carry her over."

Harry, who'd taken a first-aid class years ago as a Boy Scout, immediately vetoed that idea. "Mustn't move her. Should have left her on the floor by rights. Just leave her here on Mr. John's bed. The doctor will say if she can be moved."

If the pain had been less severe, I would have laughed at timid Harry overruling strong-willed Mayme. Maybe Harry would help keep Mayme out of John's and my hair. When Guy brought the doctor up, Jilly and Harry disappeared and Mayme motioned for John to leave the room. I indicated he should stay. Guy, who'd brought Dr. McNab up in the elevator, got the message, took Mayme's arm, and led her out into the hall to wait.

Dr. McNab shook his head when he saw my foot. "Miss James, you're some girl for getting into trouble. It's always you redheads who're accident-prone. Might have known I'd see you again soon. What happened this time?"

John took charge of answering. "She's a handful Doctor. Glennie agreed to marry me today. She got overexcited about our engagement and fell down the attic steps."

The doctor's eyebrows rose as he listened to the tale. "Somehow I doubt if that's the whole story, but it's enough to be going on with. Now tell me where you hurt, missy. Can you turn over and does that foot hurt? I hope you didn't mess it up."

"I fell on my back and it aches from hip to shoulder. But I can move, and see, I can turn over." Dr. McNab frowned when I gasped with pain. It took a couple minutes before I could speak with out crying. "My foot is a different story. I think the fall really racked it up. I could feel it hitting about half the steps as I swooped down the staircase. See all the purple's come back and it's swelling."

"Yes, if I didn't know better I'd think you'd traded your foot for a mashed eggplant. Okay, let me get out the ace bandages. We'll do the same thing as before. Stand by with ice, Mr. Fordyce." In three minutes Dr. McNab had washed his hands and skillfully wrapped my foot. "Now, no weight on the foot. Come in tomorrow about noon and we'll take another picture of it. If you've broken more bones, we'll have to go through the whole rigmarole, same as before. Do you have any of those white pain tablets left?"

"John, the bottle's on my dresser. There are a few remaining, I think."

The doctor examined my back, pressing at various points, then helped me sit up. "Take a deep breath, miss." I inhaled and felt some pain in my chest. He looked at my face and saw me grimace. "Your ribs hurt, don't they? We'll x-ray your back and chest as well tomorrow."

When John returned with my medication, the doctor gave more orders. "Give her two now and if she wakes in the night, give her two more. Are there enough to have her take two before you come to the office? No, well I'll leave you a few more." He dug around in his bag, pulled out a small bottle, and put four pills in my container. "Now young lady, you settle down and rest. Just stay in that bed till morning."

"But Doctor, I have to visit the loo. That won't wait."

"Oh, Lord." He motioned to John. "Carry her to the bathroom and BE CAREFUL! I'll see you both tomorrow."

He hurried into the hall and I heard the elevator door close. Since

Guy and Mayme had gone down to the first floor I hoped that Guy would offer the M.D. a drink for making another house call.

In the loo John stood me on my good foot and looked puzzled. "The last time we did this you were undressed. What comes next?"

"If you'll support me, I can drop my drawers. Yes, that's right. Now help me sit down easy. And hey, while I'm here, why don't you grab my big T-shirt from the closet and get me out of my clothes?" He came back in after I did my business. "I'll hold my arms up and you can pull the sweater over my head. Now drop the shirt over me."

I unhooked my bra, slipped my arms out of the straps, and let the shirt slip down farther. When my arms went through the sleeves, John stood with his hands on his hips. "What next, Glennie?"

"Help me stand and I'll unzip my skirt. See, it dropped right down. If you lift me up now, the skirt will fall off. Aren't we clever?"

"Now do you want to spend the night in my bed or yours?"

I slanted a look at him. "My bed is large enough for two." He took the hint quite nicely. Soon we'd settled under the covers with the door locked.

I moved over against him. "I'm sorry, darling, but I think snuggling is all we better try tonight. It's enough for me to be close to you. I hope you don't mind deferring making love till later."

"Of course I mind. I've dreamed of you every night for weeks. That time, after your first go-round with Ransome, when you plunked your bare bum on my arm I almost stormed your room and ravished you."

"I think I'd like to be ravished by you, John. In fact, I look forward to it in the very near future. Do you think we'll be suited physically?"

"Glennie, if you don't stop talking about it, I won't be responsible for my actions. We'll be changing the subject right now."

"We didn't have time to chat as much this evening as we'd planned. I do want to mention your mum. How do we handle the sleeping together? Do we try to hide it or brazen it out?"

"We look her in the eye and defy her. We aren't teenagers and if she's going to live here with us, we aren't going to cave into her old-fashioned morality. Go to sleep, love."

It felt so heavenly to have his warm body next to me. With his strong arms around me I could almost forget my bruised back. I wanted to spend the rest of my life sleeping with this man. In fact that is exactly what I intended to do.

When I woke the next morning a pair of warm brown eyes concentrated on me. I smiled and he kissed me. "How do you feel this morning, my little acrobat?"

"Not too bad. The pills helped me sleep well. Actually maybe I'm not wonderful, but if we can make a trip to the bathroom soon I'll feel pretty good."

We managed fine. John tucked me up in bed again and began pulling on his clothes when we heard a tap at the door. It opened just about the time he got into his pants. Mayme, in full sail, looked ready to think nasty thoughts and give us a scold.

Before she could open her mouth John beat her to it. He tucked in his shirt and pulled up his zipper. "Good morning, Mother. Glennie slept very well and is feeling some better this morning."

"I don't like what I see here. What would Lady Sheila think if she knew you two shared a room?"

"We'll never know what she thinks, because no one is going to tell her, now are they? If you'll excuse me, I'm going down to get Glennie her breakfast and fill the ice bag. See you later, Mother."

John walked out of the room and left me to deal with Mayme, who stood there with a baffled look on her face. She did not give up then but started in on me. "Glennie, what would your mother say if she knew what you were doing?"

"Mayme, I wouldn't dare tell you what my mother would say. It would shock you to the core. So we won't tell my mother either. And I'd like to point out that John and I have fallen in love and we've made some decisions as to how we're going to deal with our feelings. We think that at our advanced ages what we do, how we sleep, where we go, and how we plan our future life is our business and only our business. Now tell me what's happened with Ransome? Surely he isn't still in that bathroom."

"No, Guy came up early and whisked him away somewhere. It all happened very quietly. What will become of that awful boy?"

"If he learns to grow up, it could be the making of him. Has Guy gone then?"

"He's having breakfast."

"Mayme would you do me a great favor and ask Guy to come up and tell me goodbye? I have an idea for him that may hurry along Ransome's growing up. Please, Mayme."

She rushed away and in a few minutes I heard the elevator come creaking up its shaft. Guy tapped on the door and popped his head into my room. "You wanted to see me, Glennie?"

"Yes, I did. Have you thought of taking Ransome to an army or navy recruiter? You could stand over him while he enlists. He'd have to go where they tell him and behave, or he'd be court martialed. Tell him if he runs away and comes home, we'll call the military police and they'll haul him back again. What do you think?"

"That's a capital idea, my dear. Why didn't I come up with that? I have a car coming soon and we'll stop at a recruiting station. There should be one near the airport. Now, take care of yourself, Glenna. I'm sorry things didn't work out for us but I guess we weren't meant for each other. It's made me think more about my future."

I patted his hand. "You'll find someone, Guy. The perfect wife is waiting out there for you."

"I hope you're right. Let me know when you schedule the wedding. I wouldn't miss it for the world." He kissed my cheek and went out the door in great haste.

I lay there and thought about the end of what Mother called my big romance. Oh, yes, I'd felt an attraction to Guy at first, but it was only an attraction since the whole thing died with scarcely a whimper. Is the thing that pulls men and women together chemical, mental, or emotional? Maybe it's made up of all three. Whatever made it happen, I felt wonderful. Well, except for my foot.

I drank my tea and nibbled a scone with raspberry jam. I dozed a bit and then John bustled in to get me ready for the doctor visit. "What do you want to wear, my love?"

"I have a heavy robe in the closet. It's rather like a tent and should work well for this little jaunt. Do I have time for a shower? If the doctor is going to look me all over, I do think a good scrub would be the thing to do."

Having John help me take a shower turned out to be a lot more fun than when Mayme assisted me. He ended up almost as wet as I did. "My God, woman, you're as slippery as an eel. Don't fall. We could never explain that to Dr. McNab."

I had to laugh. "I know. It might be hard to tell the family too."

Because of my previous experience as a cripple, putting on my underclothes went rather well. I asked John to find the big roomy caftan that hung in my closet. Made of peach sweatshirt material, it went on easily. He dropped it over my head and it felt so cozy and comforting. After brushing my hair and putting on a dab of lipstick, we rode the elevator down to the first floor. Harry held the doors open and John carried me to the car.

At the clinic the X-ray technician recognized me. "Miss James, I can't believe you're back here again. We'll have your pictures in a jiffy."

A nurse rewrapped my foot and I felt like an experienced invalid when she helped me into a wheelchair. Dr. McNab had a few final words for me. "Now you know the drill, miss. Main thing is to take care of that foot since a few of the small bones broke again. You've bruises all over but nothing else is seriously injured. I suggest you spend the rest of today in bed and probably tomorrow, too. You've had a shock and rest does wonders. Just read and doze. I'll see you back here in one week."

I rather enjoyed lounging in bed with my foot propped up on pillows, ice bag in place. John or Jilly delivered my meals to me and thanks to Mayme, I didn't need to worry about my duties.

After the guests were checked in that evening, John came up with my supper. Jilly sent a mug of thick soup with rolls and butter. A dish of fruit and some biscuits finished the meal. John sat by the bed while I ate and at last we had a chance to talk about our future.

"Let's discuss the wedding first, Glennie. Do you mean it about wanting a simple affair like Jilly and Harry's?"

"Yes, that's exactly what I want. Why don't we do that and then go to Chicago for part of our honeymoon. We can have a honeymoon, can't we?"

He helped himself to one of my biscuits. "You bet we'll have one."

"Okay, then my folks could have a reception for us at Dad's golf club or some place like that. Mom would love to invite everyone she knows and throw a blast. But should we let them come to our simple wedding here? I'm really against it."

John flashed me a wide grin. "Leave them in the States. We'll have enough static from Mum without stirring your folks into the mix."

"You're right. Hey, this is easy. What's our next big decision?"

John moved my supper tray and turned back to me nonchalantly. "Would you like to buy Hollystone House from Guy? We could run it as our own bed and breakfast."

I struggled to sit up on the side of the bed. "John, how could we buy this house? What ever made you think of it?"

He put his hand out and steadied me. "It just hit me this afternoon. I couldn't wait to talk to you about it."

"But how would we buy the place? Explain that to me. It would take several hundred thousand or maybe a million pounds. But I'd love to have it."

"If your heart desires the house, we'll do it."

I looked at him sternly. "In plain English, tell me how we possibly could come up with the money."

"Glennie dear, just because I work for my cousin and am not out spanning the globe in a jet doesn't mean I'm without resources. I inherited quite a lot of money from my father and I've saved my wages like an old miser. I've invested wisely and enjoyed some good luck. We can make a hefty down payment and get ourselves a short term bank loan for the rest."

"Are you sure Guy wants to sell?"

John nodded slowly. "He said something just before he left indicating that he'd lost interest in the project. He seemed rather deflated, probably because you didn't want to marry him."

I could feel excitement at the idea begin to build. "Well, lets do it then. I also have some resources to contribute to the project. I've saved some money since I started working, plus my house is paid for, and we can sell it. In fact, we better sell it. It's appreciated a whole bunch since I bought it. I snapped it up as a derelict and restored it. We can use my money to reduce the loan principal or for operating capital. I'll invite you to reinvest it if there's any left. And right now I have 16, 000 pounds in the bank at Chartwell. I've hardly spent a penny of my wages."

John squeezed my hand. "You've overwhelmed me, Glennie. A frugal Scotsman like me certainly wants a wee wifie that can pinch the pennies. But are you sure you want to keep working? You know we could go almost anywhere we wanted. There's enough capital so that we could live off the interest or start a business of some kind."

"Someday we might decide to live in some other place, but for now I'd really like to stay here. I feel as if we have a family with the Burnses and Lady Sheila. Do you think your mother will stay too?"

"I have a feeling we couldn't tear her away. She may drive us crazy."

Making our plans was so much fun. "We've handled her so far. If you agree, I think we can keep her at bay. I'd like to have our babies all real fast before we get much older, then in five or ten years we can sell out and see the world. In the meantime we could make ourselves a nifty apartment in the south wing off the hall, I mean a really nice one. It's the only area we haven't renovated." I swung my legs up on the bed and lay back. The injured one began to throb but I ignored it.

"While you're lying there with nothing to do, start drawing up the plans. Now, one last thing. What do you have in mind for a romantic honeymoon?"

I pulled the covers up under my chin. "How about a cruise to some romantic islands or a trip on the Orient Express? We could go to Greece or I've always wanted to visit Alaska."

"I think a plan is emerging, my sweet. Let's get married in the next month. This is April. How does May sound?"

"May will be a wonderful month for a wedding."

He picked up my breakfast tray and started for the door. "Then we catch a cruise ship and drift around Italy or Spain. After two weeks we hit the States and let your folks put on their big bash. We stay there no more than three days. Then we're off to the South Pacific for another two weeks. There's a wonderful island out there called Roratonga, that's just waiting for us."

"Oh, John, that sounds fantastic. I want to leave tomorrow."

He set the tray back down and drained the teapot into my cup. "The time will pass quickly; you wait and see. And we have work to do. You and Lady Sheila can plan our tasteful wee nuptials. I'll get onto Guy about purchasing the house. We'll have to have a bit more help if we're to be gone a month. We can work on that together. Now when do we tell your folks the big news?"

"Oh, Lord, I don't know. If we tell them too soon they'll be over here underfoot. But we have to give them time to plan their party. I wonder if my friend Moira Fitzgerald would come over and be my maid of honor. I'd really like my brother to be here, but it might be too much for him to get off work and come without the folks finding out he was gone. Hey, we've done enough for tonight. I'd very much like to snuggle down here with you and sleep."

He drank the contents of the teacup and gave me a look. "When do you expect to be recovered enough for me to make love to you?"

I felt a blush rise up my cheeks. "John, I'd really like to wait till we're married. What do you think? Could you manage that?"

"You aren't a virgin, are you Glennie?"

"No, and I wish I were. I'd like to be for you. Do you mind that I slept with Guy that time long ago?"

John moved abruptly. "When was that?"

"It happened when we went to London and bought all the furniture for the house. I've regretted it ever since. I thought he cared for me more than he did. I made a big mistake. Remember the second time Guy came? When he announced that he'd put his suitcase in my room? He figured that one night gave him the right to move into my bed. He made me furious and I felt terribly embarrassed that he'd been so blatant in front of you."

"Glennie, I do mind but not that much. I'm no untarnished lover myself but if you want to wait we will. You may wake up some nights though and notice I'm gone. If I find I'm on the verge of losing control and what was that word we were using — -'ravishing you,' — I'll slip into my room for the rest of the night."

"John, tell me about your other girlfriends. Did you ever come close to marrying one?"

He picked up the tray again, started out the door, and then looked back at me. "No, I must have been waiting for you, love, and you're worth the wait."

CHAPTER 28

Our guests continued to fill the rooms in Hollystone House. They were often interesting and gracious folks. I managed to do most of my work seated in the wheelchair.

Four weeks after my spectacular crash with Ransome, Dr. McNab again pronounced me healed and I abandoned the second boot cast. After we left the doctor's office John took me to lunch at the Crown and Anchor. Over fish and chips I got up my nerve to ask him a question that puzzled me. "Tell me, if you cared for me so much, why didn't you make a move sooner? In fact, why did you leave and go to Scotland?"

"Because, Guy let me know you were his territory and told me I should keep my hands off you. When he called and told me to meet you at the airport, he made it very clear that he'd allow no poaching. He put it in such a way that I felt on my honor to keep my hands and my heart to myself. When I departed for the North Country, he made the point again. He said, 'I'm going to propose to Glenna while you're away.' Then he added, 'Do you think she'll have me?'"

"And you answered?" I stopped eating and waited for his reply.

"I didn't. To myself I thought, pray God she says no."

"Oh, John. Couldn't you sense how I felt?"

"I hoped, Glennie, but I felt honor bound to give Guy a clear field. We've always been close, like brothers, and he saw you first. There were plenty of times when I thought he'd made an awful hash of his courtship. All the time I was gone, I felt miserable. I came back determined to have you, whether Guy had declared himself or not. I decided the choice should be yours, not Guy's or mine. I'm incredibly thankful you chose me. The relief was so great I thought my heart would stop beating."

I drained my coffee cup. "Did you and guy patch things up? Is he angry with you?"

"He acted a little hurt but it looked like an act to me. Underneath he seemed relieved. I think Guy's afraid of making a commitment. I got the feeling he was keeping you on ice until he could work up his courage to take on a wife."

When we were back in the car, I had to tell him how I felt. "It frightens me to think that I could have made a horrendous mistake and agreed to marry Guy. If he'd been more suitor-like, I might have. They say providence looks after fools and lovers. Someone watched over me."

Guy called his mother to report that Ransome had joined the navy and would train at Felixstowe. It thrilled Lady Sheila that he finally done something productive. She never knew of his ghost act and we kept it that way.

John went quietly to see the Vicar about announcing the banns for our marriage. We picked a Saturday in May for the service. I put in a call to Moira Fitzgerald.

"Moira, what are you doing the third week in May?"

"Working, I suppose; who is this?"

"Don't be cute, Moira, it's Glenna. John and I are getting married and I want you to come over and be my maid of honor. Will you?" I listened for her answer, hoping against hope that she'd be there for me.

"John who? I thought his name was Guy."

"John's Guy's cousin and I've fallen head over heels in love with him."

"You've been a lousy correspondent, Glennie. The last time I talked to your mom she hoped you'd marry that Scottish lord."

"My God, don't tell her I called. Don't tell her anything. We're having a little private affair with about fifteen people. If Mother found out she wasn't invited to my wedding she'd stroke out."

"You have to tell your folks sometime. Your mother will kill you, literally, if you leave her out."

"I know we're taking a risk, but we plan to tell the folks right after the ceremony. We'll come to Chicago during our honeymoon and Mom can have a reception for us. But, Moira, I can't do this without you. Will you come?"

"I wouldn't miss it. Tell me about this John?"

I couldn't help smiling to myself. "He's the most terrific man. He's handsome and strong and I feel so safe in his arms."

"Okay, give me the particulars and I'll be there with bells on my toes or wherever they're supposed to be."

I called my brother, Michael, and bowled him over with my news. "More power to you, Glennie. I never ever want to go through the upset Mom put us through for our wedding. I really thought Sarah's mother and Mom would slug it out at the reception hall. I'm sure you remember all the fuss."

"Those memories are what decided me to do it this way."

"I'll see if I can come over. I'd love to give you away. I'll call back soon."

Because of my foot, I couldn't do much running around to prepare for the event. As soon as I could walk easily, John and I made a quick trip to London to shop. He chose a handsome black suit for the wedding. I found a cream-colored, full-skirted, long dress. Made of heavy silk it had a lace bodice and lace trim on the full, long sleeves.

Blanche, the village hairdresser, and I worked out a way to fasten a scattering of tiny white flowers and ivory ribbons in my hair. I thought a veil too fancy for our simple ceremony.

We chose our gold wedding rings and had them engraved. On John's I wanted "All My Love, Glenna" on the inner surface. John opted for "Forever Yours, John." We walked around in a sort of rosy haze as lovers have for centuries.

Lady Sheila insisted she'd provide the dinner as she had for Jilly and Harry's wedding. However, she didn't reckoned on Jilly. "You can order the cake and the drink, but I'm catering Glennie and John's wedding dinner." I left them to work out the details.

Guy promised to arrive in time to be the best man. He also agreed, after a bit of persuasion, to sell us the house. John reported that after Guy thought about our offer he called back. "The House is yours, John. I realized that with the money from the sale I could buy out a drilling company that's giving me too much competition." If I'd broken Guy's heart it had mended quickly.

John arranged the financing with the proviso that we would add the proceeds from the sale of my house to the down payment.

We revised our honeymoon plans somewhat. After the two-week cruise around Italy, we would travel to Chicago and spend two more weeks to get my house ready to sell. The things I wanted to keep would need to be packed and shipped to Hollystone. That would give my folks a month to plan the reception for us and we could still have two weeks at the end to recover in Roratonga.

Mayme and Lady Sheila arranged to raid several neighboring gardens to pick spring flowers for the church and to decorate the Hollystone dining room. Two weeks before the wedding we invited the Jardines to attend. Mayme got a wild impulse and called Jilly's fun-loving father to escort her. Guy e-mailed that he'd bring a guest and asked us to save a room for her. That wasn't a problem, as we took no reservations for the wedding weekend.

I discussed with Jilly the matter of engaging a temporary cook. She would need a hand with breakfasts and teas for the guests during our absence. "If you please, Glennie, I hear Mrs. Mayme invited me Da and he's coming for the wedding. He's a retired chef and would probably get a charge out of helping me in the kitchen while you're away."

"How splendid. John can discuss wages with him when he arrives. Should he come a few days early to get settled in with you?"

"I'll ring him tonight. I'm sure he'll be eager to come, but I'll let you know for sure."

John hired Mick and Rick Jardine to help Harry with maintenance. Mayme thought she could manage the inn with the extra help for the six weeks we'd be away.

Moira arrived a week ahead and we spent a wonderful few days recalling past escapades and laughing at old jokes. She thought John was a darling and they bantered back and forth and had great fun. She brought a flowing peach bridesmaid gown with her. I began to get really excited. John moved back to his room because the temptation became too much as the wedding day neared. God, what a wonderful man. I adored him.

Two days before our big day, Guy showed up with, guess who? Miss Yellow Curls, Annabeth Grimes, from the Las Vegas convention. I almost went into shock. I had John in stitches as I whispered in his ear, "Her clothes are made from old curtain material, I swear."

He quietly swallowed his laughter and settled down to welcome her quite nicely. She wore a suit this time but the fabric still looked as if it had come off a drapery bolt. Guy introduced her all around and she twittered like a canary, especially to Lady Sheila. Ellen thought her to be just right for Guy. She would. I heard her say to Jilly, "That Miss Grimes is a proper young lady."

CHAPTER 29

My brother, Michael, came on the same flight as Guy and Annabeth. I didn't realize how much I'd missed him. I just couldn't quit hugging him. He and John took to each other at once and that pleased me.

I loved introducing Moira to Guy. She's the most stunning girl, with honey-colored hair that swirls around her shoulders. He looked quite overwhelmed as she chatted quietly with him. Uh oh, Miss Yellow Curls, your tenure as Guy's lady friend may be quite short.

Later that afternoon, Lady Sheila called me into the parlor and here were all the women gathered for a bridal shower. I never dreamed of such a thing. Mother turned red with anger when she learned she'd missed the party.

Annabeth Grimes gave me an absolutely gorgeous lace handkerchief to carry during the ceremony. Mayme stunned us all when she presented me with a glorious set of antique garnet earrings with a matching pendant. I felt she would expect me to stick around a while before she let me have the family heirlooms. My mouth fell open when I opened the box. She hugged me and I shed a few tears on her shoulder. Jilly and the housemaids, the two Jardines wives; Betty, the sister, and Clara, the cousin, had chipped in to buy me a very sexy chiffon gown and robe set of sea foam green with blond lace trim. "It's beautiful and I know John will love it." Lots of giggling followed the opening of that present and there were a few smothered smiles besides.

Ellen frowned at such levity but unbent enough to give me a lace tablecloth she'd crocheted. She handed it over with a comment. "I knew ye'd marry either Mr. Guy or Mr. John so I started working on it as soon as her Ladyship and I moved here. Either way, I felt sure ye'd find a use for the cloth."

Moira had a lacy long half-slip and separate camisole for me. "My word, I didn't have a thing to wear under my wedding gown. I suppose at the last minute I'd have just worn a regular short slip and gone off half-dressed. How did you know I would need these lovely undies?"

"I remember you from school, Glenna. You were forever borrowing my petticoats."

The last gift I opened was a box from Lady Sheila. She gave me a pair of antique gloves that looked as if they'd never been worn. They were a creamy color and long with lace cuffs and tiny pearl buttons. They were exquisite and I am sure very valuable. "Where did you find these? They're so perfect."

"They were in one of the old trunks I had shipped here. I think John and Guy's grandmother wore them for her wedding. If I'd found them years ago, I could have used them for mine."

At that point Jilly and her dad, Bill Warrick, presented us with a lavish tea. We gobbled hors d'oeuvres, tiny sandwiches, and small white cakes with silver frosting and trim. Everything was exquisitely prepared and the assembled company fell on the food as if a famine were imminent.

Mayme had a camera and recorded the people, gifts, and tea offerings in great detail. I still enjoy going through the picture album where the shower is documented.

The men drifted in by that time, so Jilly produced more cups and they finished the tea.

On the wedding eve we slipped over to the church to meet with the pastor. He walked us through the ceremony and discussed the service. John requested that there be no "obeys." I felt so lucky to be marrying this wonderful man.

We then adjourned to the pub for a boozy and convivial dinner. Jilly's dad had a fabulous time and so did Mayme. They danced until they were breathless. The rest of us certainly enjoyed ourselves.

There were toasts and silly songs. The locals in the pub drank to our health that evening and a few of the group were awash. John drank sparingly and had wisely hired the big old village taxi to trundle the rest of the wedding party back to the inn. He and I returned in the Jaguar. We both loved the feel of swooping through the town in the long green car.

After we saw the various wedding guests to their rooms, we put the house to bed and John and I rode up to the fourth floor in the elevator. We went into my room and began to remove our party finery. All at once John moved close to me and laid his lips on mine. As he became more demanding I could feel a warm melting deep inside. He put his lips to my ear and spoke in a whisper. "Glennie, I've waited long enough. Let me love you tonight."

I looked at the desire in his eyes and knew I'd savored the anticipation of our coming together long enough. The time had come for us to move to the next level of our love. I almost answered John flippantly. Then I realized how cruel that would be. This man loved me desperately, yet he'd been patient and waited.

"Yes, John, it's time. Please love me now."

What a memorable night—one we'll both remember always. We began with kisses. The more intense John was, the more excited I became. He kissed me until my mouth burned and then the burn moved south as his lips traced a line across my breasts and down my belly. Once he lifted his head and gave me the most dazzling smile. Then he turned off the bedside lamp.

We enjoyed ourselves immensely and later cuddled close and slept deeply. Early on our wedding day, we woke and launched the day with another lovely interlude. The night before our loving had been intense, but on our wedding morn we took our time, laughing at silly things and pleasuring each other. Frankly, I could have stayed in bed till noon or later but Jilly tapped at the door and handed in a tea tray complete with my favorite scones.

We relaxed and did not hurry, but sipped the tea, and got crumbs all over the sheets. We were confident we wouldn't have to sleep there that night. We tiptoed across the hall to the original, big old bathroom and soaked in the huge tub. We finished up with a rinse off in the shower where John lovingly washed my hair.

For the first time I took a really good look at John's naked body. He had an athlete's physique with heavily muscled arms and shoulders, a flat abdomen, and great-looking legs. His chest had a thick mat of dark curly hair. I had to say it. "God, John, you're gorgeous. I can't believe you've been hiding that body under your clothes."

He blushed crimson over his entire torso and reached for a towel.

"Don't cover up. I love looking at you. Were you active in sports when you were at school?"

"I played in every event the school offered. After I got out on my own, I continued to play soccer with any team I could find. I boxed at school too, but it's soccer I love. It comes next to my heart right after you. And while we're doing all this looking over, I'm pleased to know you're truly a redhead."

My turn to blush.

What a perfect day. None of the hectic rush usually associated with wedding days. We just drifted from one little chore to another. We finished our packing. I had very little in the way of cruise wear so I planned to take an empty suitcase and buy shorts and a swimsuit somewhere along the way.

Blanche dropped by in the afternoon and fixed my hair with the tiny flowers and ribbons. Michael and I sat in the library for a while and just talked. How long had it been since I spent an hour alone with my brother? Back home there was always someone around, our folks or his children. What a special time.

"Sis, I'm so glad I came. John's a super fellow and he'll be a better husband than the globe-trotting oilman."

"You're right. I thought it would be Guy at first but I fell for John like a ton of bricks. What do you think of our buying the inn?"

"If you feel it's sound money wise, you should do it. John explained some of the finances to me yesterday and selling your house should put you in good shape. You know Mom and Dad still think you'll come back and live in Oakbrook. Speaking of them, did they cause a riot when they showed up here unannounced? You didn't give me many details on the phone."

"Did they ever! I don't know what they told you but they mortally embarrassed me. Guy arrived soon after they came and every time he or Lady Sheila appeared Mother rushed to tell them what a good cook and great little homemaker I'd be. She was so blatant and totally unstoppable. I blew my stack one night and said that they'd humiliated me enough and that they were to get out the next morning. I did not see them again but I guess John took them to the train or called a cab or something."

"Glennie, do you and John plan to have children?"

"Yes, and soon. In fact I wouldn't be surprised if last night hadn't launched our family." I grinned at him. "We better get our wedding finery on and think about going to the kirk."

We defied tradition and John drove me to the church. He pulled off on a side street and stopped to give me a tiny package. I struggled to get it open. I couldn't believe it when I unwrapped a pair of diamond earrings. "John, this is too much. Don't we need this money for Hollystone? I feel guilty having something so nice, especially after you gave me the pearls for Christmas."

"Glennie, you have to keep the earrings to wear with your gown. Don't worry so about money. We're fine. I told you I'd been lucky with investments. I expect our net worth is more than Guy's right now. But keep that under your hat. Ethically, as John's business manager, I shouldn't have told you. For heaven's sake, don't drop a hint to Miss Yellow Curls."

"I wouldn't dream of it. Do you think she has a chance? He climbed all over Moira in the pub last night, wanted to dance with her all evening. If Michael and you hadn't taken pity on Annabeth, she'd have had a dull evening. I have to say that he's recovered pretty fast from me breaking his heart."

"It's hard to say. Guy may want a little wife to cater to his every need. That isn't what I want. You're what I want, but that Moira is a stunner. She's funny too. I got a charge out of her acting like you've picked up such a British accent that she can't understand you."

"Well, soon to be husband, it's five minutes till Michael and I start that long walk down the aisle. There's such a thing as being too relaxed. Give me a kiss and let's go do it."

The minister, a young curate with a twinkle in his eye, waited for us. He gave a very moving service. There were no "obeys" but he used the rest of the traditional wording. I especially liked the way he emphasized the "till death do us part" section. I shed a few tears when John kissed me and then we sailed down the aisle as the organ thundered triumphantly. Outside the church our little group pelted us with birdseed for fertility. It was done, beautifully done and we were together forever and ever.

CHAPTER 30

We returned to the house in the green car with the village taxi doing duty for the rest of the group. Guy led us into the parlor and poured champagne for the wedding party. He raised his glass. "Glenna and John, these good folks, your family and friends and I, wish you many years of blissful marriage."

My brother, Michael, drank to Guy's toast and then stood to lift his glass. "John, you're getting a wonderful woman and I wish you both every happiness."

The entire group smiled and Mick and Rick Jardine seemed to enjoy the champagne immensely. I heard Mick's rumbling voice rise over the others. "Cheers to the bride and groom. May they have a houseful of little ones." The hall rocked with laughter after that little speech. Even Ellen drank to that sentiment.

When we could break free of our friends, Michael, John, and I slipped into the library to call my parents. Fortunately or not, they were both at home and immediately each got on a phone.

I started the conversation. "Mother and Dad, this is Glenna. I want to tell you that John Fordyce and I were married this afternoon."

The answer came back, "Who? Not that tall handsome Guy McLeod? Married, how could you get married without us? What do you mean?"

"Mother, here's John."

"Mother James, this is your new son-in-law, John Fordyce. Glennie and I said our vows about an hour ago. We're now celebrating in the great hall of Hollystone House. You can believe us, it's really true. Here's your son Michael."

Michael raised his eyebrows and took the phone. "Hello Mom and Dad. Glenna and John Fordyce are married, the wedding was charming. I'll bring lots of pictures for you to enjoy."

Mother screeched so loud we could all hear her. "Michael, how could you do this to us? Not tell us about our only daughter's wedding? I can't believe you'd do that to me. What are you doing over there?"

"I came for Glennie. She was a bride to reckon with. Now let me tell you the big news."

"She's not pregnant, is she?"

His smiling faced turned to a frown. "I won't lower myself to answer that, Mother. The good news is the newlyweds will go on a two-week cruise and then fly into Chicago. They'll spend a couple of weeks packing up Glennie's possessions and preparing to sell her house. At the end of that time you may put on a wedding reception to welcome them and introduce them to your friends. No more questions now, Mom. I'll be home tomorrow and tell you everything. We're getting ready to party and eat the wedding feast. It smells wonderful. I'll call you as soon as I'm home."

I couldn't wait to hear the folks reaction. "How did it go? What did Mom say?"

Michael drained his champagne flute and we headed back to the parlor. "Wow, is she torqued! I don't envy you, sis, when she gets a hold of you, you're gonna get it big-time."

"I know, but I'll have John to back me up and we plan to invite Mayme over for the big party. I think she'll be a match for Mom."

About that time Jilly appeared at the door. "Come away in for dinner." What a splendiferous meal. We started off with an appetizer of fresh fruit on kabobs, which we dipped into a sour-cream sauce. She served a crown-rib roast cooked to medium rare. With it were many vegetables and a heavenly mashed-potato dish that must have been full of cream. There were feather-light rolls with butter and a salad of bib lettuce and curly endive. Bill's special vinaigrette dressing made it delicious. As dinners go, we ranked it as fabulous and it made me lean close and whisper in John's ear. "If they can prepare food like this we better start serving dinners here at the inn."

Guy sat at the table flanked by Annabeth and Moira. Right then I figured the odds were fifty-fifty. Lady Sheila had a motherly grin on her face and I wondered which one she'd favor.

The wedding cake, created by Jilly's dad Bill, rested on the sideboard in all its cream frosted glory. Harry handed it down after a nod from Jilly and she gave John a silver knife with cream ribbons on the handle. As he cut slices, I held the plates for him. Jilly put a scoop of scrumptious French-vanilla ice cream beside the cake.

We'd engaged a local photographer to record the festivities and he snapped every move we made — me feeding John cake, John feeding me cake, everyone eating cake, plus all the other foolish things we did that evening.

We played CDs and tapes and everyone danced. I had several rounds with Rick Jardine. He did a mean jitterbug. I guess that was his era. I wanted to dance all the romantic tunes with John. They seemed so special. Mayme and Jilly's Pa really enjoyed the waltzes and Lady Sheila glided around the room with her son, Guy, when he could tear himself away from Moira. My brother and I showed these Brits what rock-and-roll was about. All in all, we enjoyed a splendid party. I still wonder how we danced so furiously after eating all that food.

The time came for John and me to depart. He kept on his wedding suit and I changed to a classy off-white pantsuit. Harry humped the luggage out to the Jaguar while we gave Jilly a special thank-you for her sumptuous dinner. Everyone gathered out front to see us off with hugs and kisses.

I told Mayme that she must come to Chicago for our next wedding event. "We'll be in touch about the details of Mom's party. Actually, I think Guy and Lady Sheila should come too. Rick Jardine's wife can manage the guesthouse for a week while you're away."

Guy bent to give me a goodbye kiss and I whispered in his ear. "Why don't you come to my mother's reception in Chicago? I'm sure Moira will be there." I think the devil made me do it.

He got a special gleam in his eye. "I wouldn't miss that party, my dear."

We left in the green car and drove to a luxury hotel near Heathrow.

We settled in our room and John eagerly helped me out of my clothes. I unbuttoned his shirt and he dropped his trousers on the floor. He led me to the big bed and pulled me close. "I don't know what's wrong with me. I can't get enough of you, Glennie. Are you okay? I mean I don't want to wear you out."

"I'm just as eager as you are. It's a good thing we waited till last night. If we'd started making love any sooner, we'd have waylaid each other in the library, in the halls, and probably on the dining-room table." We burst out laughing then. "Can you imagine your mother walking in while we were in a compromising situation?"

"Yes, I can. And Lady Sheila or Ellen would have been bloody awful. But forget them. Tonight it's just you and me."

He kissed me until my head swam with dizziness and took a long, slow time showing his love for me.

CHAPTER 31

We flew to Italy the next morning and spent two days in the Eternal city, Rome, before our cruise. It is truly a splendid place to visit. We saw all the usual touristy attractions. How I loved visiting the Tivoli Gardens. All those fountains and gargoyles turned me on. "John, do you think those funny little statues are sexy?"

"Right now, everything looks sexy to me. I love a rainy day like yesterday. When I woke up and saw the raindrops chasing each other down the window, all I could think was, *we can stay in bed for the whole day.*"

We had great fun going to the fabulous stores to shop. I assembled a nice wardrobe for the cruise and John was quite interested in helping me pick out a swimsuit. "Do you like the green bikini or the black one with the little-boy legs?"

"My God in heaven, Glennie, you can't appear in public in either one of them. The black one may have little-boy legs but it has a big-mama top. Let me buy you the blue one-piece suit."

"You don't have to buy my clothes. I have money."

He fingered the blue swimsuit. "Glennie, I want to buy you everything your heart desires. A few clothes barely scratches the surface of what I want to do for you."

"You're a generous sweetheart and I graciously accept. But I really like the black two-piece. Can I have that one too?"

"If you wear it only for me."

"Okay."

"Do you promise?"

I put a hand over my heart. "I most solemnly swear. Is that good enough?"

John flashed me a grin. "That will do for now, my love. Let me pay for those ridiculous wisps of cloth and we'll stop at a café for a cappuccino."

We sat on a sunny sidewalk with our sweet, creamy coffee. "You know, Glennie, you've got to quit worrying about money. We have enough."

"Which reminds me, are you going to keep paying me a salary when we're back running our very own bed-and-breakfast?"

John set down his cup. "We need to figure out things like that. We have a mortgage and will need to make hefty monthly payments. After we pay the mortgage and the expenses, whatever's left will belong to both of us. Do you think we can manage to write checks out of a joint account? It may be a challenge for two independent folks like us to share everything. I do think that when you've sold your house and car you should keep about 20,000 pounds that's just for you. The rest will be ours together. Your name will be on the deed of the house along with mine and it will belong to us jointly."

My coffee had cooled and I took a swallow. "You seem to have it all figured out. Which is fine. You've never told me exactly what Guy said when you approached him about buying the inn."

"My proposal dumfounded him at first. I explained that we really wanted to live there and run the place. It didn't take much to persuade him when I said we wanted Lady Sheila to stay with us and that Mum would also be there. I made a semi-serious suggestion that maybe in ten years we'd sell it back to him."

"I don't know why I feel so sentimental about us living there with our little family. Most newlyweds can't wait to be alone. I guess that's why we go on honeymoons."

We caught the cruise ship and lived in luxury for the next two weeks. Such idyllic days. We stayed up late to dance and slept late in the mornings. On wonderful sunny days the ship docked and we explored Naples, the Isle of Capri, and toured Pompeii. We enjoyed a stop in Sicily too. I told John all I knew about the Mafia connections in Chicago.

And we loved each other. Besides John's rainy days there were rosy hued dawns when he woke me with urgency. All it needed was a look to ignite the fires that smoldered inside us.

We had fun choosing gifts for the family. On one glorious sun-drenched day I bought Jilly a long, print skirt ablaze with color. Reds, blues, and yellows made it absolutely vibrant. And there was a matching shirt for Harry. If they appeared in the Crown and Anchor Pub in those duds, they could start a riot. But the colors would be great with Jilly's dark hair and complexion. I even picked up a couple of yards of the same fabric. Ellen would be thrilled to make wee Jamie a matching romper suit.

For Mayme, Lady Sheila, Mother, and my sister-in-law, Sarah, I bought elegant leather gloves. I never saw such beautiful work. John bought me a huge bottle of Gucci One perfume. For some reason it's not available in the States any more and I think it's the best-smelling scent there is. John liked it too.

One rainy day when we were lazing in our stateroom I called my mother. She immediately became critical, cranky and almost nasty. "Glenna, how could you do this to us? I know my friends think it's very strange that you married so far from home. And where are you anyway? I've tried to call you a number of times but you're never where you say you'll be."

"Mom, this is our honeymoon. Let us relax and enjoy it. Tell your nosy friends that you're such a busybody and so overbearing that I couldn't deal with it. That's the truth. Now stop fussing and talk sense to me. Have you set up the reception?"

"Well, of course I have, and it's been a major struggle. People make arrangements a year in advance for these events. I've set it on a Saturday night and reserved the Silver Fountain Room at the Blue Maxmillian Hotel. I could only engage the second-best caterer. The first choice was booked. You've caused me more work than you can imagine. I couldn't do the invitations until everything was planned but they're out now and people are replying."

"Wonderful, Mom. We'll be importing a few guests too. It would be nice if you sent John's mother, plus Guy and Lady Sheila invitations. Will you reserve rooms for them at the reception hotel? And I hope you included Moira Fitzgerald."

"Don't worry, dear, I went to your house and got your address book. All of your friends are invited. I believe we mailed out 350 invitations. Sarah has been a dear about helping me with them. Now, Glenna, do you want dinner or just hors d'oeuvres?"

"Dinner seems too complicated with that many people. Let's just circulate. Are you planning a reception line?"

"Well, of course, and I want you to wear your wedding gown if it's presentable. And what does John have to wear?"

"My gown is quite suitable and John's black suit is handsome."

"Now I've planned that you'll be staying with us here at home and I've reserved John a room at the hotel. Even though you're married it would look best if you're under our roof till after the reception."

I sputtered with shock at her ridiculous plans, but I should have known. "Oh, no you don't, Mother. We're properly married and John and I will stay at my house. We'll clear it out and pack my things for shipment to England. As soon as it's ready we'll put it on the market. I plan to invest the proceeds in Hollystone House, which we've bought."

"You've bought that huge barn of a building? Your father won't think that's a good idea. You better hang onto your money, Glenna. This John may just be after your investments. Have you thought of that?"

"We'll call you when we arrive, Mom. Goodbye now." I slammed the phone down as anger surged through me. That woman! How did she turn out to be my mother? Mayme could be pushy and interfering, but responded to firm requests to butt out of our business. She at least listened to reason. I could not bear to think about the meeting of the mums. It might be catastrophic. We better warn Mayme.

After that day we forgot about mothers and began to plan our home within Hollystone House. We had done nothing with the south wing off the first floor. It was a clutch of tiny rooms and for some reason Guy hadn't modernized it when he upgraded the house.

John got busy with pen and paper. "What do you think, Glennie?

How many bedrooms should we have?"

"Won't three be enough? One for us, a nursery for the children, and a guest room. If we outgrow the apartment, we'll have to annex some other rooms in the house. Surely in that huge building we can find enough living space."

Between us we came up with a good plan. It included the three bedrooms, a lounge, a small kitchen, a den, and three bathrooms. John faxed the plans to an architect friend and arranged for the final drawings to go to the Jardine brothers. It looked like they were becoming full time employees.

Two weeks of cruising in Italian waters left John with a lovely tan and my fair skin acquired a golden glow. Our cruise ended and we hated to leave Italy but more adventures waited for us. We boarded a plane for Chicago, landed there without fanfare, and took a cab to my house in Oakbrook. John liked my house and furniture. "It's a shame this entire house can't be moved to Upper Halsey. However that's out, so let's get to work and pack up your things."

First, we had to go to the folks' house for dinner. "John, beware. I'm sure Dad will get you into the study or out in his workshop for a man-to-man talk. He'll ask about your financial status and other personal questions."

The evening wasn't quite the horror that I expected. Mom seemed more interested in showing me who'd accepted invitations to the reception than carping about my unforgivable behavior.

When we came back to my house and were getting ready for bed, I quizzed John. "How did the man-to-man talk go?"

"Very well. When I showed the old boy my portfolio and impressed on him that I'm an accountant with a business degree he couldn't have been more cooperative. I think I've made it into the inner circle with your old man."

"Super. Dad really isn't unreasonable like Mother. He gets sucked up in her schemes and wild ideas, but on his own he can be a sweetheart."

I called an auction house about selling the furniture we decided not to keep. John arranged for a company to ship some of my things to Hollystone. We hauled several vanloads of stuff to the Salvation

Army and by the day before Mom's party we had the house empty and clean. I listed it with a realtor and signed the necessary papers so I could avoid returning for a closing.

We shouldered our bags and moved to the Blue Max Hotel. We then drove my van to O'Hare and met our British guests, who looked quite perky considering the long overnight flight.

They rested at the hotel and then my parents, Michael and his family, and Moira Fitzgerald joined us there for dinner later that evening. We made sure to seat Mayme and Mom far apart. Lady Sheila and Guy helped keep the conversation upbeat and on safe topics.

Guy found time to pay Moira lots of attention. I thought she'd be perfect for him, but forced myself not to meddle. It was tempting though. I did wonder what became of Miss Yellow Curls, but had sense enough not to ask. My mother would have pounced on it.

"Moira," Mother piped up, "Will you wear your bridesmaid gown to the party tomorrow night? Glennie's wearing her dress and it would look so nice."

"Certainly, Mrs. James. It's been cleaned and is ready for your party. Did you get a new dress for the reception?"

"Oh, yes. It's an aquamarine crepe with a drape on one side. And Lloyd bought a navy suit. I wanted the men to wear tuxedos but Glenna put her foot down. I don't know what I did to deserve such a heartless child."

I thought for a minute that Mayme was going to challenge that, but John winked at her and she settled right down.

CHAPTER 32

I woke the next morning with an elephant size case of jitters. John quickly ordered tea and rolls sent to our room. "I can't believe you're this nervous, love. You were so relaxed at our wedding. What's happened?"

"I don't know. I guess its uncertainty. I feel as if Mom has a surprise up her sleeve. She'll probably have a thousand white doves released in the middle of the party and I just can't stand that kind of showiness. I'll try to calm down. We should be thankful she didn't make Michael put on a bachelor party for you. They're drunken orgies with girls leaping out of cakes and belly dancers doing their stuff."

John smiled fondly at me. "The only belly dancer I want to see leap out of a cake is you. Can you arrange that?"

"Not until after Mom's reception. I'll check into it after that." I drank three cups of tea and girded my loins for a busy day.

First, Mom's friends had a brunch for me and collectively presented me with eight place settings of the most expensive china I've ever seen. It was beautiful but Mom chose the pattern. I felt dreadfully embarrassed when I opened the big box. Too much is too much.

After the brunch I managed a brief nap and then my old hairdresser came to put the tiny flowers in my hair. No ribbons this time. Moira came to my room, as we'd decided it would look good for us both to wear the flowers. Then we couldn't do much for fear of messing up our hair.

As the time approached to get ready, butterflies played catch in my stomach. Mom wanted to come to the hotel to "help me dress." I said, "No, John will help me." And he did lift my dress over my head so as not to disturb the hair-do.

Mom slated the reception to begin at seven o'clock and we were to be on tap thirty minutes before hand. John and I showed up fifteen minutes late because I figured fifteen minutes would be all we could stand of mother's micromanaging. She lined us all up, including Michael and Sarah. Guy, Mayme, and Lady Sheila had to have someone to introduce them to each guest. I could see this going on for hours.

John took Mom aside and gave her the word. "Mother James, you may introduce my aunt as Lady Sheila McLeod, but we do not say Lord Guy. Guy doesn't use his title at all and would be unutterably embarrassed to hear it spoken." The bad news almost brought Mom to her knees but she rallied. She did make sure she stood by Lady Sheila so she could use, lady, the magic word.

After the first seventy-five people arrived and made it through the reception line, I began to calm down and relax. By that time I could see tension building up in John. He leaned close to me. "How many more people are coming?"

"Hundreds, dear. Just hang on. And look at that table over against the wall. It's heaped with packages and see that waiter setting up another table for presents. I had completely forgotten that all these folks would bring gifts. It'll take us forever to open them and we have to write thank-you notes for all of them. We should open them before we leave for the South Pacific. In fact, mom won't let us out of the state until we've unwrapped them."

"You mean all these folks had to bring presents?"

"Well, they didn't have to, but it's the thing to do. Mom and I've given gifts to all my high school and college classmates when they married. And she's bought presents for the children of her friends from church and women's clubs, plus Dad's lodge brothers. It's a sort of reciprocal thing."

John's tan paled a bit and I hoped he'd hold up till the end. Finally the line slowed to a trickle and most everyone had a drink and a plate of goodies.

I forgot to mention that on the buffet table there was an enormous wedding cake. When the last person straggled through the reception line, Mom herded us to the table. She thrust a silver knife decorated with ribbons into John's hand. Mom's photographer stayed right on the spot as John cut a bite and fed it to me. I returned the favor and one more thing could be crossed off Mother's list. We strolled away and waiters cut and served the rest.

"I don't think I thought things through. If we'd had the folks come to Upper Halsey, we could have avoided all this hassle. Oh, well, it'll be over soon."

How could I have been so wrong? About this time a five-piece musical group arrived and set up to play for dancing. So we danced — me with John, me with Dad, me with Michael, and me with Guy. All duly photographed. Then John led out his mother, my mother, Lady Sheila, Sarah, and Moira.

The high point of the evening wasn't white doves, but a waiter pulled a rope and a net up at the ceiling let down a thousand white balloons. They drifted down on the dancers, hit some of the hot lights and popped, and caused much confusion. I picked up one and it said John and Glenna on it with the date of the party, not the day of our wedding. I handed a balloon to John. "See, I told you she'd do something tacky."

By midnight my feet felt fried and John had turned pale again. But people started drifting away and Mother assured us it had been the party of the season.

Next, General James, as John and I were privately calling mother, ordered the men in the wedding party to start hauling gifts down to our various cars. John stepped up and took charge. Oh, this man I married couldn't be more wonderful. "Dear Mother James, stop right there. We aren't hauling these things anywhere. I'll rent the room for tomorrow, and after we've all had a good night's sleep we'll gather and open the boxes. Then the Pak Mail shippers will come right here and rewrap each item for the trip overseas. I'll arrange it now and have the room secured and locked. We'll meet here for a breakfast at ten o'clock and have an orgy of opening." It pleased me to see that John could handle Mother and get her to back down on something.

His idea made wonderful sense and I really think Mother felt too tired to argue. The down side was that she wouldn't be able to display the gifts at home and invite her friends over to view the haul while she gloated.

We stripped off our wedding finery for what I hoped was the last time and fell into bed. John rolled over toward me and gave me a ribald wink. "I never dreamed how many wedding nights we'd be enjoying. What do you say to a quickie this time?"

I sputtered with giggles. "Is that longer or shorter than a nooner?"

John shook the bed with laughter. "Glennie, don't ever stop amazing me with your smart remarks. But please save them just for me."

I solemnly promised and by that time we'd revived enough that quickies and nooners were summarily replaced with slow, dreamy lovemaking.

We didn't open an eye until nine in the morning. John got up and called Guy to ask when their return flight left. I looked across the room and noticed a funny expression on his face. He talked a while and then came over to me with a grin that stretched from ear to ear. "Guess who answered the phone?"

I thought and then couldn't help but squeal. "Moira! Moira answered the phone, didn't she?"

"Yes, seems Guy's showering, but he'll call me back when he's free."

We burst out laughing and became almost hysterical. We leaned on each other and roared. I managed to say, "I hope my mother doesn't decide she needs to speak to Guy about something and call."

We calmed down and dressed. When we arrived at the Silver Fountain Room for the great unwrapping of the gifts, I noticed that Moira must have come prepared. She wore a stylish pants outfit and looked like a blooming rose. I really hoped she wouldn't show up wearing last night's dress. I need not have worried. Moira knows what is appropriate and what is not.

With ten of us toiling like beavers for at least six hours, we got through the mountain of gifts. Mother did the recording and the rest of us ripped paper. Lady Sheila and Mayme were stunned at the largesse. From behind a mound of paper I heard Mayme's voice. "I doubt Charles and Diana received this many gifts."

I encouraged her to photograph the heap of tributes. There were six bedspreads, fourteen sheet sets, and enough towels that we could avoid doing laundry for five months. We tallied china pieces, which when added to the earlier gift, would seat twenty-four at table. People gave us a boatload of lead crystal, plenty for a banquet. The appliances piled up and none of them were for the United Kingdom's electrical system. We returned them before we left Chicago and traded for a video camera and a set of sterling silver.

Mayme and Lady Sheila continued to be shocked at the haul. Mayme commented in a wry voice. "I didn't dream you'd get this much stuff. I have a pathetic offering for you back home. I polished up the Fordyce Georgian silver tea set to pass on to you. I hope you'll have room in your cupboards to store it." I gave Mayme a hug and told her I was thrilled with the gift.

Lady Sheila gave me a small smile. "You didn't get a teapot. Not a single one. I'm sure they'll be glad to use the family silver, Mayme."

The group broke up and we found ourselves going to dinner with Guy and Moira, also Michael and Sarah. Mother and Dad took Mayme and Lady Sheila for a meal so we youngsters, as she called us, could have a last visit.

Our dinner waxed rather nostalgic as we talked over some of the funny or nice things that happened at both the British and the American versions of the wedding. Sarah pushed aside her dinner plate. "I so wanted to come with Michael for the ceremony. I just didn't see any way to leave the children without Mom James finding out I'd gone. I told them Michael had gone away on business and believe me when the news came out, your mother grilled me about that. Now she thinks she can't trust me."

John motioned to the waiter to clear the table. "Once we're back at Hollystone, you'll have to bring your family for a nice long visit."

Michael and Sarah spoke together. "We'll come."

Afterward we went back to the hotel and said our goodbyes. The Brits planned to leave early in the morning and we wouldn't see them again. Our plane for Roratonga left at noon and we had a busy morning before that. We were uncertain but thought it looked as if Moira again went with Guy to his room.

CHAPTER 33

In the morning we exchanged the gifts, and made final shipping arrangements. Our last task took us to a car dealer, who would sell the van for me. I could hardly believe I'd wound up my Chicago life. It seemed like the way floodwaters wiped out a town. There wasn't a sign I'd ever lived in the windy city. In two weeks John and I totally obliterated my former existence. I had no idea when I would ever be back. Frankly that felt good.

The flight to Roratonga took a long time but we dozed, nibbled mediocre food, and talked. "How do you know about this island where we're going?"

"When I served in the army, they sent me to New Zealand. From there we could fly to Roratonga for R and R. I remember it as having a beautiful climate, gorgeous beaches and none of the usual touristy nonsense."

"Tell me more about it."

"Well, I've reserved us a rustic cottage right on Muri Beach. We can roll out of bed and into the ocean."

"Do we stop to put on swim suits?"

"When I went there before, you could skip right out in the altogether. There may be more people around than there were then. Besides they were all men on that visit. I think we should proceed with caution."

We moved into a very secluded cottage. We compromised by wearing terry cloth robes to the water's edge and then making speedy leaps into the surf. It turned out to be the best two weeks of our lives. Some days we slept late and walked the beaches in the evening. Other mornings we arose early and walked the beaches at dawn. We swam and napped; we ate fruit and drank juices at all hours of the day. John became very darkly tanned and I certainly added more freckles.

There were people around to say hello to, but mostly we stayed to ourselves. One evening we ate dinner at the main lodge with another honeymooning couple. They were considerably younger than John and I and seemed totally bemused with each other. They had stars in their eyes and held hands between courses.

Back in our cottage, we laughed about them. "Do you think we're that conspicuous?" I asked.

John's eyes twinkled as he pondered the question. "No, love, I don't. I worried that it would all become too much for the fellow and he'd have a go at her right there on the table."

We enjoyed the dinner but we didn't feel the need to dine with others again.

There was no television or radio. We just spent time together. We talked about our childhoods. John told me about his father, also named John. "He died when I'd just turned sixteen and left a great hole in my life. I felt cast adrift for a while after Dad passed away. I didn't know what to do or how to plan my life. My Uncle George, Guy's father, had died only the year before. We were left hanging but we supported each other and eventually got on with our lives."

I talked about the great summers Michael and I had when the folks moved us to Lake Michigan for the season. "Back then our family seemed different. Before puberty came along we didn't have to listen to talk about finding a mate. There were no lectures about being a good girl. We just lived in the water and enjoyed being kids."

There were days when, after we'd talked ourselves out we made slow and dreamy love. Some nights our cottage sizzled with hot sex. John would look at me with those melting brown eyes and I could not throw my clothes off fast enough. Time simply stood still and we felt enclosed in a glass bubble.

There was a small chink in the bubble when I realized that I should have had a period by this time. We were splashing in the surf when it hit me. "John, John, I think I'm pregnant. I'm overdue and I'm always on time. Do you suppose I really am?"

"Well, you've certainly been exposed enough to be expecting. This is what you wanted, isn't it?"

"Oh, yes. We've got to find a pregnancy test kit. I wonder if they sell them in one of the hotel shops?"

After two glorious weeks our idyll was over. It took very little time to pack as we'd worn only shorts and swimsuits, which were sandy and damp. We dumped them in plastic bags and would worry about washing them when we got home. Home was Hollystone House in Upper Halsey. I felt so ready to be there.

Our homecoming was quite joyful. Harry fetched us from the airport in the green car. He'd picked it up there after we flew away. Our silent handyman chattered his head off all the way back. "Jamie's grown so big you won't know him. Getting even more hair too. It's still dark like Jilly's. He tries to say Da for Dad. Mick and Rick have started in on your apartment. They've pulled out the old walls of those bitty rooms. It's just one big space now. They're anxious for you to take a look at the plans and make sure everything is right."

The rest of the family stood in a line at the door as we drove up the drive and there were hugs all around. Jamie acted afraid of us at first, we'd been away so long. The Jardines hovered anxiously, wanting to report on their stewardship of the house and to consult about the apartment. They surrounded us in a babble of sound.

Jilly announced that the tea tray waited in the morning room and we should "Come away in."

While I had my mouth full of scone, John answered questions about where we'd been and what we saw and did. Then Lady Sheila gave us her news. "Guy and Moira Fitzgerald are practically engaged and we think she'll come here in the fall. Wedding plans are up in the air but we believe they're committed to each other. There was talk of them buying back the dower house from you, John." What a thrill to think of Moira being nearby. I'd been so busy working that I'd made no friends in Upper Halsey, only Jilly.

Finally, when things calmed down and we were into our second cups of tea, I told our wonderful news. "I'm pregnant."

Mayme flushed with excitement. "Are you sure, Glennie, really sure?"

"Yes, I'm sure."

Lady Sheila looked a little sad but managed to give us a smile. "You must be so pleased."

"We're thrilled." John slipped his arms around me from behind, held me fast, and dropped a kiss on the back of my neck. We were home and a lifetime of love and exciting adventures were ahead of us.

A CAN OF MAGIC SMILES
by Elizabeth E. Rogers

Grandma keeps a can of magic smiles in her cupboard. Her grandchildren think the can is empty, until Grandma puts a smile on her granddaughter's face from the can. Grandma time is very special time to children.

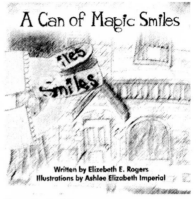

A Can of Magic Smiles

Written by Elizebeth E. Rogers
Illustrations by Ashlee Elizabeth Imperial

Paperback, 28 pages
8.5" x 8.5"
ISBN 1-4241-8671-4

About the author:

Elizabeth E. Rogers has lived in Central California most of her life. Having been born in Arkansas, she has a strong Southern influence. Learning the art of story telling from her grandmother, Emma, she draws wisdom and strength from the traditions she was taught. She says her grandmother was the perfect role model. Elizabeth has been writing short stories since she was a child. The children in *A Can Of Magic Smiles* are her own grandchildren. Elizabeth is the mother of five children: three daughters and two sons. Elizabeth's daughter is the one who urged her to write some of her stories. Two of her daughters have myotonic muscular dystrophy. She is raising one of her grandsons, who also has muscular dystrophy. Now single after a 23 year marriage and just starting her career as an author of children's books, *A Can Of Magic Smiles* is her first published work. Drawing inspiration from everyday life and her family, Elizabeth plans to continue writing children's books. She says writing allows her to be creative and stay at home to care for her children.

Also available from PublishAmerica

COME AND MEET BACI

by Diana Granata

A story told by Baci, an Italian Greyhound, sharing his ancestry, personality, characteristics and traits of being a royal dog. Baci believes that to love where you come from and enjoy your individuality is what makes each of us special.

Paperback, 39 pages
8.5" x 8.5"
ISBN 1-60474-463-4

About the author:

A 30-year resident of Connecticut, I still retain a fondness for my birthplace and true "home" — Italy. Choosing Baci, my Italian Greyhound, brings me closer to my roots on a daily basis. My desire to share information on my native country and the chance to respond to children's curiosity about my dog's breed, prompted me to write this book. Please enjoy and learn.

Available to all bookstores nationwide.
www.publishamerica.com

THE COCKAMAMY WORLD OF A. YOLD

By Paul Mackan

I first met A. Yold in the dumps. I was down there for—well, that's for another time. Two guys meet in the dumps, they're Canadian, they talk! It's a national characteristic. "Strangers in the night?" Not if they're one of us. Now I am one kind of Canadian; Yold is his kind. Anyway, thinking seasonally, I said, "Are you having a happy Easter?"

"Easter-shmeester," he said. "I'm a Jew." It was the start of our friendship.

It felt funny addressing him as "A" all the time, but he wouldn't tell me what name the initial stood for. All he'd say was, "So you should hear it from me; my mother is unorthodox." And after a pause, while I couldn't think of a thing to say, he lowered his head and smiled. "She's the original Hadassa bizarre." And I was in love—do not infer.

Paperback, 81 pages
6" x 9"
ISBN 1-60610-055-6

About the author:

Paul Mackan lives in Ottawa, Ontario. He's an award-winning writer, broadcaster, and film maker. He's the widower of Sara Lee (Harris) Stadelman, to whom he remains single-mindedly committed. He does film and stage work, and is a member of both Alliance of Canadian Television and Radio Artists, and Canadian Actors' Equity.

WHY I AM A COUNSELOR
by Anthony A.M. Pearson

Why I Am a Counselor is a powerful and painful story about a little boy's journey into the darkness and what he learned. It is about overcoming, persevering, discovering purpose, and about liberation and success! Inspiring all who have heard it, it is a true story about a spiritual-psychological awakening that brought about an empowered, authentic life. It explores the questions:

• What forces can take a sickly, fearful, abused child and empower him to become a minister, teacher, and counselor of excellence?

• What is a counselor, and what was the journey that led the author to become a counselor?

• What beneficial life lessons can be drawn from the myriads of counseling theories?

• Can a spiritual-psychological collaboration benefit human existence and the counseling profession?

• How do humans reach maximum potential?

The author hopes that this self-revelation will inspire others to make their own journeys, overcome challenges, and understand their purpose in life.

Paperback, 133 pages
5.5" x 8.5"
ISBN 1-4241-9186-6

About the author:

Anthony A.M. Pearson is an ordained minister, educator, counselor, teacher, historian and motivational speaker. He was trained in theology, history, and counseling psychology. He is married, with five sons and nine grandchildren. A recipient of numerous honors and recognitions, he is founder of **Winds of Change Institute**, a human-potential organization.

THE 1776 SCROLL

By Louise Harris

Living alone in Philadelphia, 19-year-old Charlie Schofield struggles to repair the shattered relationships in her life while fighting for her spot in the Magical Strike Force Academy. She takes up with a lonely friend who secretly knows that Charlie is in danger. An evil wizard plots against Charlie over powerful magic locked in a scroll. When Charlie cannot open the scroll to release the magic, the wizard hatches a new plan to discredit her in court using more conventional means: she's to prove herself insane and the scroll a hoax. Will Charlie unlock the magic in the scroll before the wizard goes free? Will she prove that she was the victim and not the perpetrator of a crime? Or will the court decide that she is nothing more than an attention-grabbing witch? It is a race against outer forces and inner demons.

Paperback, 104 pages
6" x 9"
ISBN 1-4241-5098-1

About the author:

Louise Harris aspired to write since her youth. She published her first poem at age 12, wrote her first song at age eight, and became an editor. *The 1776 Scroll* is her first novel. Louise lives in Arizona with her husband, three children and two cats. Her heart remains in Philly.

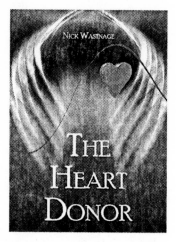